Veronica Moon is married, and lives in Twickenham. She went to Farnham school of art and then worked in advertising for many years, before pursuing her interest in antiques; learning to restore china. She has had a handful of poems published and her previous novel *The Scent of Honeysuckle*. She loves animals, nature, history and boozy lunches with friends.

Best wishes
Veronica Moon.

I dedicate this book to my lovely husband, and to my old English teacher, Mr Chamberlain-Andrews, who gave me my love of literature.

Veronica Moon

OUT OF THE DARK

AUSTIN MACAULEY PUBLISHERS™

LONDON · CAMBRIDGE · NEW YORK · SHARJAH

A CIP catalogue record for this title is available from the British Library.

ISBN 9781528992886 (Paperback)
ISBN 9781528992893 (ePub e-book)

www.austinmacauley.com

First Published 2022
Austin Macauley Publishers Ltd®
1 Canada Square
Canary Wharf
London
E14 5AA

Many thanks to my dear friends, Heather Morgan, Gillie Spargo and Helen Blackburn, for their help and encouragement.

Chapter 1

Jessica had almost finished entering the last few names into the ledger when the lights went out. "Damn!" she swore under her breath and was almost tempted to finish off by torchlight so that she could claim the full hour of overtime, but she knew that the management would know exactly what time the power had gone off and would never accept it. They paid by the half-hour, and she was damned if she would give them any more of her time for free.

Sighing deeply, she closed the ledger and stretched, easing her aching shoulders. Things took so much longer these days because of the constant power cuts, and the firm now insisted that everything had first to be entered into a ledger before being transferred onto the computer. Previously, people had lost names and addresses when the power unexpectedly went off if they had forgotten to save the data, so now it all had to be put down on paper first.

She opened her desk drawer and groped for the powerful torch, and then putting on her coat and pulling on her hat, she grabbed her shopping bag and hurried downstairs where the porter was waiting impatiently to lock up. "'Night!" She called, quickly signed out and then opened the door into the darkness of the street. Her bag was a little heavy, as it contained not only her groceries but her son, Josh's, Christmas present.

She had been so lucky to see it in her local charity shop window, and the woman had told her that she had only just put it in. It was a compendium of games that consisted of chess pieces, draughts, dominoes, and a set of cards; all complete and still with the instructions, and in almost pristine condition. She smiled when she thought of Josh's face when he opened it on Christmas morning. They would be able to have hours of fun over the holidays and she imagined her husband, Sam, teaching him the rules of chess while she would prepare their food. Jess had asked Sam what Josh had wanted most for a gift and he had replied, "Oranges." They were now very hard to find around their village, and so she had bought a bag of oranges and two lemons, and she decided she would get another bag tomorrow when she had less to carry.

The wide street was in pitch darkness, and it had started to become foggy, and she was fearful of having to cross it, so she waited in trepidation at the kerb to pick her moment to run over to the other side. The traffic lights were not working at the crossroads, and without the streetlights, it was difficult to gauge the speed of the vehicles, especially the bicycles. Some of the riders rode two abreast, and from a distance, appeared to be motor cars. At last, she managed to find a gap in the traffic and ran across the road, and just narrowly missed being hit by a cyclist who was riding without lights, and swore at her loudly.

She turned right at the crossroads and then had to walk about a mile to reach her flat, and on her way home, she would pass by the derelict factory where the feral cats lived. Every morning, on her way to work, Jessica would take them some dry cat food, and there was one beautiful cat, a black tom, that had taken a particular liking to her and often let her stroke him through the bars of the gate, but if she tried to entice him out he would beat a hasty retreat. She would have loved to have taken him home, but he was the king of his patch, the dominant male who did not want to leave his harem. Most of the cats were abandoned pets that people could no longer afford to keep, or whose owners had been made homeless. Some people admonished her for feeding them, and she had been sworn at and ridiculed. "Why waste your money on those creatures? They can live on the rats." She had been told several times, but some of the cats were elderly and could no longer hunt for their food, and she cared about them and did not want them to starve.

Once, she had been yelled at by a woman who had seen her throw a bag of dry food through the gates. "You're a disgrace!" The woman had shouted. "You could be giving that money to a homeless person." Jessica did give a generous percentage of her wages to a charity for the homeless, but what she spent on the cats was not even enough to feed a man for the day. Anyway, it was her money to spend as she saw fit, so rather rudely she told the woman to: "Mind your own effing business!"

Now, as she reached the high wall of the factory compound, she heard footsteps behind her, turned quickly but could see nothing through the thickening fog. She was always nervous along this stretch of road at night, as there were no houses nearby and she felt vulnerable and exposed. Her heart was beating ten to the dozen, and quickening her pace, she hurried on, but the footsteps also quickened. They were gaining on her.

Suddenly an arm grabbed her roughly around the throat and a man's voice said hoarsely, "Give me your money." Jessica cried out, "Let go! Leave me alone, I don't have any money!" Although she normally kept a ten-pound note in her purse for emergencies, today, she had spent all it on Josh's present. She could smell the cheesy, unwashed smell of him, making her want to gag, and his arm tightened around her throat as she struggled to break free. "What's in the bag?" he demanded, but Jessica gasped and begged, "Let go please, I can't breathe!" All of a sudden, something dark flashed past her face, and then the man gave a startled cry and abruptly dropped his arm.

It was the black tomcat. Leaping down from the high wall, it had landed on his shoulder and sunk its claws fast into his neck. He was in pain and swore loudly, and attempted to pull the cat off, and so Jess used the opportunity to break free and ran as fast as she could, not stopping until she reached the safety of her building. She unlocked the door with shaking hands and collapsed at the bottom of the stairs, trying to catch her breath.

Almost at once, the door of the ground floor flat opened and old Mrs Trent emerged, holding a candle in her shaky hand. "Is that you Jess?" she enquired, peering blindly into the darkness, and when Jessica affirmed that it was, she told her that she had a letter and a parcel for her.

"Oh Gertrude, can I come in for a minute please. I've just been attacked outside the old factory, and I'm feeling a bit shaken up."

Gertrude gasped. "Oh no! You're not hurt, are you?" Jess shook her head. "No, but my heart's thumping. It was terrifying." Following the old woman into the flat, she told her how one of the feral cats had saved her from the attacker. "That's Karma dear," Gertrude told her. "You look after them and they look out for you. Now, I can see how upset you are, so would you like a cup of tea? It's still hot, I just managed to boil the kettle before the power went off."

"Yes please, that would be lovely," Jess said gratefully.

She was still shaking as Gertrude poured the tea into two cups from a china teapot swathed in a thick woollen cosy. "My Grandma knitted this," she told Jess proudly, "and it's almost a hundred years old and keeps the tea warm for ages."

She added a drop of milk and handed a cup to Jess who sipped the hot liquid with gratitude.

Gertrude smiled and asked, "Are you feeling better now dear?" and Jess nodded and told her, "It's delicious tea, thank you, and I'm feeling quite alright now."

"I make the tea with proper leaves," Gertrude told her with pride. "No teabag rubbish, and though it costs a bit more, I can use the leaves twice." Jessica agreed and said, "Yes, tea is very expensive now, I suppose it's the cost of shipping it all that way from India." A dreamy look crossed Gertrude's face and she said, "I went on a ship once for my honeymoon. It was a cruise around the Mediterranean. Oh, it was lovely! All the food and drink you could want and seeing all those sights without even having to move from the comfort of your cabin."

"It must have been wonderful" – Jess agreed wistfully – "but sadly those days are long gone." She had never been abroad and could only imagine the luxury that Gertrude had experienced. When she had married Sam, they did not have enough money to honeymoon overseas and had instead spent a long weekend in a bed-and-breakfast in Brighton.

Gertrude sighed. "It's such a shame for the young people now, they'll never have the experiences that we had, will they? We took everything for granted, didn't we?"

"Yes, but we were brought up in a very wasteful society and we didn't know any better," Jess said. "We all had a mobile phone and a computer or tablet that connected us around the world, and no one ever counted the cost, did they?"

"Yes, we did squander so much" – Gertrude agreed sadly – "but no one could have foreseen the future, could they? We were positively encouraged to do everything electronically."

Jess had been born in 2010, and by 2039 everything was beginning to unravel. Large areas of Northern and Eastern England and the Somerset levels were having to cope with flooding frequently, and then insurance companies refused to pay out to people with homes in those areas, so that they eventually had to give up and move away to higher ground. Many then became homeless because there were not enough affordable homes to go around, and landlords charged exorbitant rents. There were very few jobs for them either, as much of the more mundane work had all been taken over by robots, and there were not enough skilled jobs to go around. Young people had been positively encouraged to go to university, but once they had got their degree many found that they could not get jobs to match their skills and had to take anything that they could find. Many just dropped out of society altogether and took to drink or drugs, and suicide among the young was at an all-time high.

Jess had trained as a computer programmer designing websites, and she had loved her work. She had met her future husband, Sam, on a dating website, and she had been immediately attracted by his sweet smile and his open, boyish expression. She had never known what it was like to be part of a family, as both her parents had been killed in a road crash when a lorry had jack-knifed on the motorway. Jessica had been in the back, strapped into her baby seat, and she had somehow miraculously escaped with only minor bruising. She had grown up in care, and she was not very adept at making friends, but she had always longed to have a husband and a family of her own. As she was then in her late twenties, she thought that she had better do something about it, and so she began to try to find a mate via her computer.

Her first few dates had been a disaster, and she wondered why men bothered to lie by supplying photographs that were ten years out of date, or give vastly different ages or weight when, as soon as you met them, you were bound to be disappointed. One of her dates had put that he was fit, active, and interested in all kinds of sport, but when he turned up, he was at least twenty-five stone with an enormous beer belly. She wondered if perhaps he had made a few typing errors, and it should have read fat, inactive, and interested in watching all kinds of sport.

Another of her dates had seemed promising when he arrived, as he really did look like his photo and had even taken the trouble to dress smartly. Sadly, he had nothing to say for himself. They had spent an excruciating couple of hours over an indifferent meal when neither of them could think of a single topic of conversation. They could not wait to take their leave of each other.

She had almost given up with the computer dating, but then Sam's smiley face popped up. He had beautiful blue-grey eyes and short brown hair with a slight curl, but it was his cheeky smile, with the hint of a dimple in his cheek that attracted her. She thought she would give it just one more try. They had arranged to meet in a wine bar, but he had been a few minutes late, and she had thought that it was not a good start, but then he turned up, apologising profusely, and explained that he'd had to show a client around a property, and he had simply taken ages. "I couldn't very well throw him out" – Sam told her – "but I kept looking at my watch and eventually he got the hint and took his leave."

"So, you're an estate agent?" Jess asked, and added, "You didn't say what you did on your profile."

"Well, a lot of people think of us as leeches, but it's a decent job, and I like showing people around." He grinned and said, "I'm just nosy really; I love to see how the other half lives." Jess thought how refreshingly honest he was, and Sam had immediately liked the look of her. He had always been drawn to slim, dark-haired women, he did not know why. She fitted the bill, and he liked her calm, intelligent demeanour, and the fact that she seemed interested in him and was serious about meeting someone and not just dating for fun.

He smiled at her and asked if she wanted to eat there in the wine bar or go to his favourite Chinese restaurant that was just around the corner. She opted for the Chinese but said, "You'll have to enlighten me on some of the food as I'm a bit ignorant, and the only dish I know is chicken chow mien."

Sam decided he would order several different courses so that she could try them all, and then he encouraged her to attempt to eat with chopsticks, assuring her that it was easy once you got the hang of them. At first, she was pretty hopeless, but then he took her hand and positioned the chopsticks correctly. After a little practice, she was quite comfortable using them. When he had touched her hand, Jess had felt a little frisson of electricity pass between them and wondered if he had felt it too. There had been some sort of a spark, and so she decided to ask him, "How come that a smart, nice-looking young man like you has to resort to using internet dating?"

"I'm glad you think I'm nice-looking" – he laughed – "and the compliment's returned by the way, but I never seem to meet the right girls for a serious relationship. All the girls at work are either married or engaged and when I go clubbing, the girls I meet just want a good time."

"I know what you mean" – Jess agreed – "I almost gave up, but now I'm glad I didn't."

"I'm glad you didn't too." Sam smiled and then looked around for the waiter so that he could pay the bill. He went to get their coats and later when he had walked her back to her flat, he had kissed her, and then she had been smitten.

They had made love on only their second date. Jess had chosen to go to an Italian restaurant that she knew, and over dinner, Sam told her that he had grown up in the countryside on his father's smallholding. "I was an only child, as my parents left it quite late to start a family, and after I was born my mum couldn't conceive again. I wasn't lonely though, as I had plenty of friends and pets, and I used to love going exploring on my bike. Sometimes, I'd come home with a basket of blackberries, or hazelnuts, or wild mushrooms that we'd found."

Jess was more than a little envious and said, "You were so lucky! What on earth possessed you to leave your lovely home and come to London?"

"A sense of adventure, I guess," Sam told her. "A friend had found a job in London and asked me if I would like to go too. We decided to share a flat, and then I got lucky and found my job at the estate agency. But what about you?"

"Oh, I don't have a family," Jess said sadly. "I grew up in care getting shunted from one foster family to another. I suppose I just became a bit of a nerd really, spending all my time on the computer." Jess had always felt that she was ugly as a child. She was thin and leggy, and her straight dark hair was cut in an unflattering style. She also had to wear braces, and so never smiled if she could help it, and she got a reputation for being sullen. Her last foster mother, Elsa, had understood and told her that she would be beautiful in a couple of years and was merely going through the ugly duckling stage that many children experienced, boys as well as girls.

"You're not pretty Jess" – she told her – "but you are beautiful and have good bone structure, and as you get older you'll appreciate that." She had been the only person until she met Sam, who had loved and valued her, and Jess had been devastated when she became ill and could no longer care for her.

"Didn't any of the families you stayed with want to adopt you then?" Sam asked.

"Oh yes, there was one couple. They were really kind, and I would have loved to stay with them, but unfortunately, when I was fifteen, Elsa, who fostered me, became ill and was diagnosed with cancer, and she died a few months later."

"That must have been so hard on you," Sam sympathised.

"It was" – Jess sighed – "and I guess I just shut down after that." She was grieving, and so she had behaved in a pretty wild manner for a time, not caring what happened to her. In her wild rebellious stage, she had got a tattoo of a butterfly on her shoulder, dyed her hair with brilliant green streaks, and got her nose pierced. This she came to regret when she got a streaming cold and found that frequently having to blow her nose was rather painful. She got rid of the nose ring after that, and thankfully the hole it had left soon closed up.

She had slept with quite a few rather unsavoury characters, the latest of whom had introduced her to cannabis. Eventually, when he had tried to get her to smoke crack she had come to her senses, as she had seen the awful damage that this one drug, in particular, could do to people. One evening, her so-called boyfriend's squat was raided by the police, and as luck would have it, she had gone out to the corner shop to get something to eat. On her return, she saw the police cars parked outside and the inhabitants being led out in handcuffs, and so she turned on her heel and never went back.

It was a time in her life that she was deeply ashamed of, and from then onwards she decided that the single life was preferable, and so she just concentrated on honing her computer skills until she was competent enough to find a good job that she loved.

A short time before she met Sam, she had been lured by an eager salesgirl in one of the department stores and persuaded to have a complete make-over. When the girl had finished plucking, creaming, and painting her face, Jess had been amazed by the result. She saw that she did look beautiful in the mirror, and in gratitude, she bought all the creams and make-up that the girl had suggested. She never quite managed to achieve the same effect, however, but it was a great improvement on her previous look. Now she had far more confidence, and she realised that her biological clock was ticking, and so felt the need to have a stable relationship and start a family before it was too late.

Sam went to pour her some more wine, but as she reached for her glass she clumsily knocked it over, splashing the red liquid all over Sam's clean shirt. "Oh my God, I'm so sorry!" she cried, and tried to mop it up as the waiter came to her rescue. "It needs to be washed out before the wine dries," she told Sam. "Come back to my flat and I'll rinse it out for you." He didn't need any more encouragement, and as soon as the bill was paid they hurried back to her apartment.

As luck would have it both her flatmates were out, and as Sam stripped off the ruined shirt she could not help but admire his well-toned body. Quickly, she soaked the shirt in the sink and scrubbed at the red wine marks with soap and stain remover and was relieved when they began to disappear. She hung it over the bath to dry and offered Sam one of her sweaters to put on while it dried, and then she made coffee and put on some music.

Sam told her some more about his childhood but then eventually looked at his watch and said he had better go, so Jess went to fetch his shirt, but it was still too wet to put on. He had followed her, and as she turned around he suddenly pulled her towards him and kissed her, a long lingering kiss that made her melt. "Do you really have to go?" She asked softly, and when he hesitated she took hold of his hand and led him to her bedroom.

They made love slightly awkwardly in her single bed, and afterwards, he fell asleep straight away, but Jess lay awake for quite a while listening to his regular breathing and inhaling the clean, masculine scent of his skin. She watched as his eyelids fluttered, lost in a dream, and the hint of a smile appeared on his lips. She wondered if he was dreaming about her. She realised that she was falling in love with him, and she hoped that he also felt the same way about her.

The next morning when Sam awoke, he didn't know where he was for a moment or two, and then he turned and saw Jess sleeping beside him. He thought that she looked rather vulnerable so that he felt the urge to protect her, and the feeling surprised him, as he had never felt that way about a girl before. Her oval face in repose was that of a Madonna, and with her heavy-lidded eyes fringed by long, dark lashes and her dark hair spread over the pillow, he thought she looked very beautiful. She was smiling slightly, perhaps at something in a dream, and so he planted a soft kiss on her lips and then she woke up, stretched, and asked, "What time is it?"

"Nearly eight o'clock. The time I was up and off to work."

"Okay, I'll make tea and get you some breakfast," Jess said, pulling on her dressing gown, but he said, "There's no need. I'll get a coffee and a roll on the way to work."

"I'll just go and fetch your shirt," Jess told him, and she was relieved to see that it had dried without a trace of the red wine stain remaining. "Would you like me to run the iron over it?" She asked, but Sam shook his head. "No, it's fine as it is. Shall I pick you up on Friday? There's a good new band playing at my local pub, and we can grab a bite to eat first." He kissed her before taking his leave, and she would have liked nothing more than to drag him back to bed, but she would just have to be patient until Friday night.

Their relationship blossomed and then Sam, while working at the estate agency, had the opportunity to enable him to snap up a small two-bedroom flat when properties were at a premium. It was a chance too good to miss because affordable accommodation in the city was like gold dust. He phoned Jess and asked her to view it with him. The flat was on the first floor of a Victorian conversion and consisted of a large lounge incorporating a kitchenette, two bedrooms, and a bathroom, and everything badly needed re-decorating. "I wouldn't be able to afford it on my own," he told Jess, "but if you were to move in with me to share the cost it would work out okay, or…" He hesitated, suddenly tongue-tied.

"Or what?" Jess asked.

"Or maybe we could get married."

Jess gasped in surprise and asked tentatively, "Sam, is that, by any chance, a proposal?"

"I guess it is." He grinned, and dropping on one knee asked, "Jess, will you marry me?"

"Yes, of course, I will!" Jess laughed delightedly. "And I love the flat. Let's buy it!"

She had moved in with him after a few weeks and they had great fun choosing colour schemes to decorate and furnish their love nest. With both her and Sam working they could easily afford the mortgage and they got married in the Spring of the following year. They had agreed to wait a while before starting a family, as while both were earning good money they wanted to save enough to buy somewhere with a garden for their children.

Then Jess became pregnant, and though unplanned, they were both delighted. In 2039, she gave birth to their son, Josh, and after much discussion, they had agreed that once Jess's maternity leave was up, Sam would give up his job to look after the baby. "It makes sense, Jess," Sam had told her. "Because you're earning far more money than I do."

Chapter 2

It was a few months later, on a Saturday morning, in August, when something momentous happened. The weather at the time was sweltering, with no sign that it would break, and the heatwave had lasted for three weeks already, and people were fed up. Tempers were short and nearly everyone was hoping for a storm to bring some much-needed refreshment to the dusty cities and the parched countryside. Jess was taking a shower and washing her hair, and Sam was preparing breakfast while Josh was happily kicking his legs in his Moses basket. Sam turned on the TV to listen to the news and was stopped in his tracks as the announcer gravely said, "We have some breaking news. Sometime in the early hours of this morning, the Channel Tunnel has been blown up. Police believe it was the work of a right-wing extremist group, but so far no one has come forward to take responsibility."

"Jess!" Sam called, "Come quick!" Jess, thinking that there was something wrong with Josh, leapt out of the shower, quickly wrapped a towel around herself, and dashed into the kitchen.

"What's happened?" She asked in a panic, but seeing Josh happy in his cradle she calmed down and sat down next to Sam. "Someone's blown up the Channel Tunnel," Sam told her, and she looked at him in disbelief and asked, "Who would do such a terrible thing? Was anyone killed?" He shrugged and said, "I don't know. They're showing the entrance at Dover now." They both sat glued to the TV until a smell of burning alerted Sam that the toast was ruined, and he got up to switch off the grill. Nobody yet had any idea of the extent of the damage, but it transpired that luckily no one had been hurt. A reporter on the French side of the Channel said it was completely blocked at their end of the tunnel too, but until engineers had done a full inspection, no one could tell how bad the damage was, or when it would reopen.

They were glued to the television for most of the day, and the news when it came, was bad. The extremists had made a thorough job of destroying the Tunnel, and engineers said it would take years and billions of pounds to repair. As a result, almost overnight the price of air travel and ferry tickets went up, as passengers now had lost the rail option to cross over to Europe.

Then, after a couple of years, more changes occurred, with many well-known companies going into liquidation, and the computer company that Jess worked for went under too, and everyone was made redundant at a moment's notice. She tried very hard to find another job in computing but nothing was going. She needed the money, and so she began to look for any job that paid a living wage. She found one within walking distance from their flat, but it was with a loan and debt-collecting company, and although the wages were fairly good, she hated what they stood for and having to work for them. She was offered a contract of either five or ten years and, after discussing it with Sam, she opted for the ten-year contract as well-paid jobs were becoming harder and harder to find.

The government had introduced the contract system some years previously as a means of safeguarding people's employment. The old zero-hours work patterns had meant that someone could lose their job for no good reason and consequently would be unable to keep up with mortgage payments or their rental agreements. It was a good scheme in some ways, but if you wanted to leave a company before your contract was up, then you had to pay them 25% of the salary you would have earned. Likewise, if the company wanted to let you go, they had to do the same, unless of course there were serious grounds for dismissal.

Then everything changed dramatically when the oil in the Middle East began to run out and OPEC decided they could no longer export oil but would keep what they had for themselves. The USA had not been affected that much, as they could produce enough fuel for their own uses, but Europe was badly hit and would have to rely on buying oil from Russia at exorbitant rates. Petrol became severely rationed, and those people who had invested in electric cars were congratulating themselves on their foresight but were due for a nasty shock. Now all those electric-powered cars, that the government had actively encouraged people to invest in to cut pollution from the cities, were left rusting away by the roadside.

The fracking that the British government had introduced, much against people's wishes, in the twenties, had exhausted the supply and had finally come to an end. The upheaval of the earth had caused a lot of problems with sinkholes suddenly appearing and flooding happening where previously there had been none. Then, there was more devastating news. The newly erected nuclear reactor that had been built under a lot of protests, and was to service London and the surrounding area, had to be shut down owing to a serious fault, much to the government's embarrassment. No one had a clue when, or even if, it would be ready to go into production again.

Now fuel, to run the manufacturing companies, was having to be severely rationed, and whereas natural energy was being harnessed wherever possible, it wasn't nearly enough for the country's needs. Some people had wisely invested in solar panels, and they were the lucky ones, and Sam's father had been one of them. However, there were many thousands who could not afford to install them or whose properties were not suitable.

Power cuts were happening every day now, mostly when the working day was at an end and people were heading home. All unnecessary use of power was banned, and all streetlights and advertising signs had been permanently switched off as a means of saving energy. Nobody could use their home computers anymore, and those who tried to get around this by charging their mobile phones or laptops at work were heavily fined. However, the landlines were still working as the government had realised that people needed some form of communication to use in an emergency. So many companies had gone under, especially those that relied too heavily on the use of the internet, and it seemed that every week another well-known name went to the wall.

Television companies that had previously run programmes continuously for twenty-four hours were now only allowed to broadcast for a maximum of eight hours a day. The channels had to drastically cut back on a number of their features, and as a result, many people in the entertainment industry lost their jobs.

It was not bad news for all companies, however, and many profited from the loss of fuel, mainly bicycle manufacturers, candle makers, and any articles that could be powered by batteries, especially the ones charged by solar power. People began to read more, now that they could no longer access their mobile phones and laptops, and sales of books rocketed. People were forced to stay close to home, whether they wanted to or not, as the electricity cuts made it very difficult to travel at night. Their local pubs benefitted from the increase in customers. Many landlords decided to put on some sort of entertainment, and consequently, there was suddenly a demand for acoustic guitars and brass instruments that needed no electricity, and breweries began to make a healthy profit as a result.

Chapter 3

After her ordeal with the mugger, Jess relaxed and gratefully sipped her tea as she showed Gertrude the compendium of games that she had got for her son and said thankfully, "I was so lucky to find this, and I'm sure that Josh will love it."

"You must miss him," Gertrude replied, and Jess sighed. "Yes, you can't imagine how much." Gertrude nodded and said sadly, "Oh I think I can, my love; I haven't been able to see my boy for years."

Jess had forgotten that the old lady had not had any news from her son in Australia and she was at a loss for words on how to comfort her. So, she took out the bag of oranges and said, "Can you believe that this is what he wanted for Christmas, bless him?" Gertrude looked longingly at the oranges and Jess, catching her look, asked, "Would you like one?"

"Yes please, if you can spare one. It's been ages since I had an orange." She began to peel it and sniffed appreciatively, saying, "Oh, it always smells like Christmas to me." Jess suddenly felt very sorry for the old woman and asked her what she was doing over the holidays.

"Nothing much" – she shrugged – "my friend, Alice, might pop around for a bit of tea if she's on her own."

"Why don't you come and spend Christmas with us at the cottage?" Jess said impulsively. "We've got a spare room and plenty of food." But Gertrude shook her head and said, "That's lovely of you to offer, dear, but I haven't been outside for years, and I don't intend to start now."

Gertrude Trent suffered from agoraphobia which had got worse over the years until she could no longer leave the building. She used to do all her shopping online, but since the power cuts started, she could no longer do this. Her weekly food shopping was now done for her by a local charity. However, the shops they used only had very basic supplies, so the orange was a very welcome and unexpected treat. "Have you got my post?" Jess asked and got up to gather her things. "Oh yes, here it is." Mrs Trent handed her a parcel, and she was gratified to see that it was the book she had ordered for Sam. It was about foraging for wild food and was filled with recipes and information, including how to make wine. She had also bought him a bottle of brandy and two bottles of good claret, which together had almost cost her a week's wages. It was a special treat for Christmas that they couldn't get in the village. They would both savour it over the holidays.

Once Jess had closed the door, Gertrude Trent sighed and poured out the last dregs of the teapot. It tasted a bit stewed, but at least it was still warm. She would have given her right arm to be able to take up Jess's offer of Christmas in the country, but she found it impossible to leave the house. Lord knows she had tried to go out with her friend, Alice, but the feelings of panic simply overwhelmed her until she thought she would pass out.

She remembered fondly the day Jess and Sam had moved into the upstairs flat and introduced themselves. They had been very much in love and full of hope for the future, and it had reminded her of that time with her first husband Roy and brought back all the feelings of how excited they had been the first time they had bought their house together. When baby Josh arrived, Sam and Jess's happiness had been complete, and Gertrude was delighted with the arrival of a new little life.

Jess had been a rather nervous mother, a little unsure of caring for a new baby at first, and had often knocked on Gertrude's door to ask her advice, as she had no mother of her own to rely on. The old lady had been glad to help, as she knew she would never have grandchildren of her own, and little Josh became a surrogate grandson to her. Eventually, Jess had been obliged to go back to work, and then Sam had stayed at home to look after the baby. Gertrude would sometimes cook him some lunch, and in return, he would reciprocate by doing a few odd jobs about the place, such as putting up a shelf or unblocking the kitchen sink. He had asked her once why she never went out, but she didn't want to tell him the real reason and just told him that she suffered from her nerves.

Gertrude would often babysit for them, and she remembered the first time Jess had tapped at her door to ask her. "Mrs Trent, Sam and I would like to go and see a film at the Odeon on Friday, and we were wondering if you'd consider baby-sitting? We'd pay you, of course."

"Don't be silly Jess," she had told her. "I don't need paying, and I'd be delighted to look after little Josh. And please call me Gertrude, as calling me Mrs Trent makes me feel old."

As Josh grew older, Sam would sometimes leave him with her while he went shopping, and one day she had a terrible fright. She had left her front door ajar so that she could listen out for the postman as she was expecting a parcel. The front door had not been closed properly and a gust of wind had blown it open. Suddenly, quick as a flash, little Josh had toddled out and into the road and Gertrude began to run after him. He, of course, thought it was a game and began running further, but Gertrude screamed, "NO Josh!" And he, hearing the panic in her voice, began to bawl at the top of his lungs. He just stood there, screaming, so she had to gather all her courage to run out and scoop him up and bring him safely inside.

Her heart was pounding, and she felt sick, but somehow, she had managed to pull herself together and calmed him down. He soon forgot the incident and was playing happily with his toys when Sam came back from the shops. However, it had really scared her and brought home to her just what could have happened, and she made sure to always keep her door firmly shut, in the future.

As Josh grew older he would spend most every afternoon with Gertrude, and their childish games of snap gradually progressed as she taught him how to play rummy and cribbage. Sometimes, she would get out her photo album and show him all the places that she had visited on her cruise, and he could not get enough of her stories. She thought, sadly, that he would probably never get to visit any of those places, but she hoped that maybe one day things would improve, and life could continue as it had for all those years previously.

Gertrude missed her son, Peter, dreadfully and wondered what he and Wayne would be doing. Maybe they would be spending Christmas on the beach in Australia, but why hadn't he written? He must know how much his letters meant to her, and she couldn't help but worry that he'd had an accident. She pushed that thought to the back of her mind and focussed on Josh instead.

He had been the light of her life for eight years. His company was something to get out of bed for and to look forward to each day. She had watched him grow, helped him with his homework, and answered an endless stream of questions. She would have loved nothing more than to see his joy on Christmas morning when he opened his presents, but it was just not possible. Suddenly, she began to weep, great gulping sobs, as she realised that her life now had no purpose or meaning anymore.

Jess, meanwhile, now hurried upstairs to her flat and turned on the radio. She unpacked her shopping and wrapped Sam and Josh's presents and then settled down with her supper to listen to the evening play. Supper was just a simple cheese and pickle sandwich, not her favourite, but it was a safer option as chicken or fish could go off very quickly once the power for the refrigerator failed.

She had intended to phone Sam, but she was still rather shaken up after her ordeal. He would sense that all was not well with her, and she didn't want to worry him. She missed him terribly and would have given anything to feel his comforting arms around her, but he would feel guilty that she had to face the dangers of the city on her own. He had always made a point of meeting her from work once it got dark, and had he been there, she would have been safe.

The play was rather good, a murder mystery, and it helped to take her mind off her ordeal with the mugger. Once she had eaten, she got undressed and took the radio to bed with her where it was warmer, and when the play was over, she turned off the radio to save the battery and blew out the candle. She would try and get another bag of oranges tomorrow and give them to Gertrude for Christmas. She also resolved to get up early to wash her hair and dry it with the hairdryer if the electricity was on again in the morning.

Chapter 4

Just before Josh's eighth birthday, Sam had received a distraught phone call from his father to tell him that his mother had been taken to hospital and was feeling very unwell. "You know what she's like, Sam," he told his son. "I had to force her to go and see the doctor."

"Dad, what's wrong with her, is it serious?" Sam asked with concern, but his father replied, "They don't rightly know, and they're doing all sorts of tests. She wants to see you and little Josh, can you come down right away?"

"Of course. I'll get the train tomorrow. What hospital is she in?" His father then told him, and he began to pack a small holdall for him and Josh, and when Jess got home from work, he told her what had happened. "Sam, of course, you must go," she told him. "Your dad needs your support, but why do you have to take Josh?"

"Mum wants him to come, and I got the impression it's not good news, so it might be her last chance to see him."

"Okay then, I'll let the school know. How long do you think you'll be away?"

"I don't know, for a few days at least, I should think."

When Sam got to his parents' smallholding, his father was distraught and told him, "She's been diagnosed with Lyme disease, Sam, and they've also found cancers in her liver, and they say there's nothing they can do for her now. She should have visited the doctor earlier, but now it's spread, and it's too far gone."

"How on earth did she get Lyme disease?" Sam asked, puzzled, as he had always thought that it was caused by a rat bite.

"I reckon she was bitten by a tick while out walking the dogs, and she never realised at the time." He brushed a tear away from his eye and said, "I always wear me boots when I take the dogs out, but I've seen her a few times go out in just sandals and bare feet."

"Poor Mum, we'll go to the hospital this afternoon," Sam told him, "and maybe Josh will be able to cheer her up a bit."

His mother rallied a little when she saw him and Josh, but she was bright yellow with jaundice and looked terrible. "Why is granny that funny colour?" Josh asked, but he was too young to understand so Sam just said, "Oh she's probably been eating too many sherbet lemons," which were Josh's favourite sweet, and the explanation made him giggle. Sam kissed his mother and made a rather unwilling Josh do the same. He stayed with her for about half an hour, holding her hand and talking to her about their home and how Josh was doing at school, but her eyes kept closing, and eventually, Josh became restless and wanted to go.

"Take the car back to the farm," his father told him. "I'll sit with her through the night, and I'll call you in the morning, and don't forget to shut up the chickens."

Sam's mother passed away during the night and his father was lost. "I don't know how I can go on without her," he said forlornly. Sam didn't know how to comfort him, but it was

Josh, whose persistence managed to drag him out of the house that made him pull himself together. They went together to feed the chickens and collect the eggs, and then dig up some potatoes for their supper, and just doing these normal tasks with his grandson helped him to cope with his grief.

After the funeral, his father asked, "Can't you and Jess and the boy come here to live with me? The house is far too big for me on my own."

"Yes, Daddy!" Josh crowed. "Please let's stay here. I want to live here with Grandad."

"Dad, we'd like nothing more than to move here, but you have to understand that Jess is tied into her contract for another three and a half years. There's no way we could afford to buy her freedom." His father's face fell, and he said, "I understand Son, and I wish I could help you with the money, but I just haven't got anything left after the funeral expenses."

"We'll come and see you as often as we can," Sam promised him. He made sure to phone his father every week and often the old man was reduced to tears. "I don't know what to do without your mother, the place is just so empty without her," he told Sam. "Can't you come down and see me?" he begged, and Sam agreed to visit him within ten days, but then Josh caught chickenpox and he had to cancel his trip.

It was a couple of weeks later that the police called around at the flat to tell Sam some bad news. "We're very sorry to be the bearers of bad news Sir, but I'm afraid your father's been found dead."

"Dead? But how? Was it a heart attack?" Sam was stunned, as he'd only spoken to him a few days before, but when he was told that his father had taken his own life. He was overcome with anger and guilt. "One of his neighbours found him hanging in the shed," the officer told him, "and they tried to resuscitate him, but I'm afraid it was too late." Sam's legs went from under him, and he had to sit down. "Thank you for letting me know," he said. "I'll get the morning train down tomorrow."

When he had got over the shock he went downstairs and knocked on Gertrude's door. He needed to talk to someone, and she was always there. "Sam, come on in." She welcomed him. "Would you like a cup of tea?" He nodded and then burst into tears. "Whatever's wrong my love?" She asked with concern, and then he told her that he'd just heard that his father had hanged himself. "We were supposed to visit a couple of weeks ago, but then Josh was ill, and I had to cancel. Why couldn't he have just waited till half term?" he said angrily. "I would have brought Josh to see him, and he was so excited to be going back there."

"Well, he was probably suffering from depression, and it's such a terrible illness Sam," Gertrude told him. "It's hard to understand, but it's as if you're down in a dark pit and you can't see any way out. He must have missed your mum an awful lot."

"He did, but that's no excuse for killing yourself, is it?"

"Maybe he'd just had enough of the struggle and wanted to be with her. You mustn't blame yourself," Gertrude told him. "After all, even if you'd been able to visit when you planned, who's to say he wouldn't have done it at a later point?"

"I suppose you're right" – Sam conceded – "but I'm just so angry. He was the only grandparent Josh had left, and Dad knew that he was so looking forward to seeing him again." As he drank his tea, he mulled over how he was going to break the news to him, and then he looked at his watch and realised that he was going to be late to pick Josh up from school and said, "Sorry Gertrude, I've got to dash."

Sam hurried up the road and as he reached the corner, he saw his son waiting at the school gate looking around anxiously for him. A car had stopped nearby, and to his utter amazement, he saw a woman get out and try to drag Josh into the back of the vehicle. "Oi!" Sam yelled at the top of his lungs. "What the hell are you doing with my kid?" He ran as fast as he could, and Josh clung on to the railings for dear life, but the woman was determined to take him and only let go once Sam had reached them. Giving him a mouthful of abuse, she jumped back in the car, which sped away, and Sam was too shocked to take down the number and was trying to comfort Josh, who was by now crying his eyes out. On their way home, he decided he would not tell him about his grandfather's death. He'd just had a terrible shock, and so he would prepare him gradually by saying that Grandad was ill, and he was going to look after him. Then, after a suitable amount of time had passed, he would break the bad news to him.

When Jess got home from work, he waited until Josh was in bed before telling her about his father's death. She had known that something was amiss, but he had told her instead about the incident at the school gate. She was horrified and angrily urged him to be careful in the future and never to be late again. Later on, when she found out the real reason, she hugged him and apologised. "Oh Sam, how awful for you. I'm so sorry. What will you do now?"

"I'm going there tomorrow and will be staying for the funeral. I'll tell Josh that his grand-dad's passed away in a day or two. I've told him he's ill, so he'll be a bit more prepared."

"Look, it's half term next week. Why don't I take a couple of days sick leave and then bring Josh down to stay with you?"

"That would be wonderful. He so enjoys feeding the chickens and playing with the dog."

The next morning, before work, Jess knocked on Gertrude's door. The old lady was still in her nightclothes, and Jess apologised for disturbing her so early and said, "You know what happened to Sam's father, don't you?" Gertrude nodded, and Jess said, "Well, Josh was nearly abducted at the school gates yesterday, so I daren't let him go back today. Sam's leaving to catch his train in an hour, and I wondered if I could leave Josh with you till I get home from work?" Gertrude was horrified at the attempted abduction, as she had heard on the radio that children were being stolen and sold as slaves, and so she said, "Of course, you can leave him with me, I'd love to have him, and he'll be quite safe here." Jess was relieved and asked Gertrude not to tell him that his grandfather was dead. "Sam will tell him in a couple of days, and I'll be taking him there on Saturday so that he can spend his half term on the farm."

Sam's boyhood home was in a village on the edge of the Cotswolds, and the stone cottage stood on three and a half acres of land. His father had kept a few chickens and grew some fruit and vegetables and had sold the surplus eggs and produce, but he had earned his main living by doing odd jobs around the area. When Sam arrived, he found that the house was in a bit of a state as his father in his state of depression had not felt up to keeping the place clean. The house was weather-proof however, and there was plenty of wood to burn in the stove, so he knuckled down to getting the place clean for when his wife brought Josh down to visit.

Jess took Josh down to the farm at half term and Sam had asked her to bring along his dark suit for the funeral. As soon as they arrived, Josh wanted to run inside to see his grandfather, but Sam stopped him. "Joshy, I've got some very sad news to tell you. You remember I told you that Grandpa was ill…?" Josh nodded and then, seeing Sam's solemn expression he asked, "Is he dead too, just like grandma?"

"Yes son, I'm afraid he is. He's gone to be with grandma now."

"And are they happy now and are they looking down on me from heaven?"

"Yes, I'm sure they are," Sam reassured him, and Josh replied, "Well, that's okay then, but I will miss him. Can I still go and feed the chickens?" Sam was filled with overwhelming relief at the matter-of-fact way that Josh had taken the news, and said: "Yes, of course, you can." He had expected him to dissolve in floods of tears and be inconsolable over his grandfather's death, but he had simply accepted it in the same stoical way as that of his grandmother.

Over the next couple of days, Sam had long and tearful conversations with Jess over the matter of what to do about Josh. "I just can't risk leaving the cottage empty, you know that squatters would move in here in no time, and then we'd never get them out," he had told her. "I think it would be better and much safer if Josh lived here permanently with me, and then you could come down and stay as often as possible."

"I know, but I don't think I can bear to be without both of you," Jess had wept.

"But you know what happened at the school gate?" Sam reminded her. "How are you going to ensure that it doesn't happen again?"

"I…I don't know." Jess had not thought it through. She often had to work late and no one would be able to pick him up and bring him home. She knew it would make sense to leave him with Sam, and he was so happy here playing with the animals. It would break her heart to leave him behind, but in the end, after much heart-searching, they had both agreed that he should stay there with Sam. He simply could not risk leaving the cottage empty now because of the high probability of squatters moving in, and the city had become a dark and dangerous place, with so many jobless, homeless people roaming around that they had begun to fear for Josh's safety.

The incident of the attempted abduction had made up Jess's mind, and although she would miss him dreadfully, she knew it was in the boy's best interest to stay with his father. In the countryside, she knew that he would be safer and healthier, with the air not so polluted from all the fires that were being burned in the city. She had discovered that there was a good school that was within walking distance from the cottage. Jess knew it was for the best, but she was nonetheless distraught. She would not be able to see them for almost three months when she would be entitled to take her holiday.

Chapter 5

When Sam and Josh had moved to the countryside, Jess had felt utterly bereft and could hardly drag herself out of bed in the mornings. The flat was so quiet, and she missed Josh's cheerful prattle. Now there was constant silence, sometimes broken by the sound of canned laughter drifting up through the floorboards from Gertrude's radio. She was a little hard of hearing and had the sound turned up quite high. Even the road outside was quiet, with only the occasional car passing by, and if it wasn't for her radio, she would have gone crazy.

Jess didn't have many people in her life, only one really good friend, Amelia, who she had met at college. They chatted on the phone once or twice a month. The next time that Amelia called, she soon realised that something was wrong. Then it all came pouring out, how much Jess was missing Sam and Josh, how much she hated her job, and how lonely she was feeling.

"Look, it's your birthday next week," Amelia said, "so why don't I treat you to lunch at the Wallace?" The Wallace Collection was housed in a small museum in Manchester Square, which was just a few minutes' walk from Selfridges department store. Amelia had a job designing the museum's brochures to publicise the wonderful collection of paintings and porcelain. She also had to catalogue all the exhibits. It was a job that Jess had envied, but now she was very glad that she didn't have to do the daily commute into central London, as she hated travelling and only went there occasionally.

The museum had a courtyard in the centre that had been covered over by a glass roof, with strategically placed flowering shrubs and small trees growing in pots. It had been made into a restaurant that served delicious food, and it was an oasis of calm in a busy and not very safe part of the city. Jess loved it there, but she told Amelia that she would have to work on her birthday.

"Tell the old bastard you've got a dental appointment or something" – Amelia laughed – "and then take the day off for once."

"Alright then, I'll do it," Jess agreed. "Shall I meet you at midday, at the restaurant?" It was all arranged, and she cheered up at the thought of seeing her friend again and of the lovely meal that awaited her, and also the chance to look around the museum once more.

The day before her birthday, Jess timidly approached her boss and said, "I'm afraid I need to have tomorrow off as I've got a hospital appointment."

"Bit short notice, isn't it?" He snapped.

"Well, I only received the letter yesterday."

"What's the appointment for?" Her boss asked curiously.

"They've got to run some tests," Jess lied.

He sighed and popped a toffee into his mouth and then said, "Okay, I suppose I'll have to put you down for a day's sick leave." As she turned to go, he quipped, "Not dying, are you?" Oh, she was dying alright. Dying to give him a good slap around the chops, but instead, she smiled sweetly and said, "I hope not."

The morning of her birthday dawned bright with a mellow autumn sun, promising a pleasant day ahead. As she opened her cards from Sam and Josh, they phoned to wish her a happy birthday. She would have given anything to be able to hold them in her arms. She told them that she was being treated to a lovely lunch by Amelia. Just as she was eating her breakfast, there was a tap at the door, and it was Gertrude with a card and a small gift for her. "Come in, I've just boiled the kettle," Jess said. "It's so good of you to remember my birthday."

"Well, I've got nothing else to occupy my mind, have I?" Gertrude smiled. "I do hope you like the scarf. It's real silk and it's one I used to wear when I went out somewhere smart."

"It's very beautiful," Jess told her, "and so kind of you." It was in shades of red, orange, and yellow and it would suit her dark looks perfectly. She poured Gertrude a cup of tea and told her about her lunch invitation, and Gertrude said, "If I give you the money, would you be kind and get me a book from the museum?"

"Yes, of course, I will," Jess said and then asked, "What sort of book would you like?"

"Anything with lots of pictures," Gertrude told her. "I do like looking at beautiful things, but I can't go out to places anymore now." When she had gone, Jess put on her smartest dress and carefully made up her face, but then covered herself up with her old shabby coat as she didn't want to draw attention to herself. As it was such a lovely day, she decided to take the bus into central London instead of the tube.

As they neared Marble Arch, she was horrified to see that Hyde Park had been turned into a cardboard city, with many, many homeless people dossing down under any makeshift shelter they could find. Some were already under the influence of drink or drugs, and she was reminded of a Hogarth etching from the eighteenth century entitled 'Gin Lane' where the destitute were on the streets in various states of inebriation from cheap gin. She got off at Selfridges and in the doorway, she saw a dishevelled beggar who was holding out a tin can for alms.

There was something familiar about him, and with a shock, she realised that he was a famous character actor who had at one time appeared in virtually every soap on television. If he had sunk to this level of degradation, then what hope for the rest of them? Quickly she opened her purse and took out a ten-pound note and pressed it into his hand. "God bless you, madam," he said. "Thank you for your generosity."

"No, thank you for all the wonderful characters you've played," Jess replied. "You were one of the best." A tear rolled down his cheek and he nodded and said, "You recognise me then?"

"How could I not? You were on TV every week, what happened to you?" He shrugged and said, "There are just not enough parts to go around now that they've cut the viewing times. I was ill for a while and couldn't work, and now they only want to employ new faces."

"Well, I hope your luck changes soon, God bless." Jess hurried on, but she was shaken to think that someone who had been so successful was now on the streets. If it could happen to him, it could happen to anyone.

She was a little early for her lunch date, so she went first to the museum shop to choose a book for Gertrude. She picked one with many more pictures than text because Gertrude had confided that she now had difficulty in reading for long periods. Amelia was waiting for her in the restaurant and greeted her with a big smile and a hug. "It's so good to see you, Jess. It's been far too long." She had ordered a glass of Prosecco for them while they perused the menu. Jess felt relaxed and happier than she'd been for a long time.

As they were eating, she told Amelia about the actor she had seen who was down on his luck and her friend nodded in sympathy. "I know, it's awful. Just last week someone from the Royal Opera House was begging in Covent Garden, literally having to sing for his supper." They soon changed the subject and Amelia asked how Josh was doing at his new school. "He loves it, and he's made quite a few friends. It's much safer for him too." And Jess proceeded to tell her about the attempted abduction at the school gate. "Oh, if I could only win the lottery" – Jess sighed – "I'd kiss goodbye to that horrible job and be on the next train out of here!" Amelia smiled sympathetically and asked, "How is the fat controller?"

"Vile! He just gets fatter, and it's all from poor people's misfortune. I don't even think he's a human being." After they had drunk their coffees, they had a brief tour around the museum, but Jess wanted to be home before dark, and so she took her leave of Amelia and hurried to get the tube from Marble Arch.

The platform was already busy, with quite a few people heading home early. Suddenly there was a commotion and a filthy, ragged man with bare feet stumbled along the platform shouting abuse at everyone. He was high on drugs, and people dodged out of his way as best they could. Then, to everyone's horror, he shoved an unsuspecting man over the edge of the platform just as a train was due in. The man, who was elderly, just missed hitting the live rail, but he was bruised and shaken and could not manage to climb back onto the platform. The rails started to hum with the approach of a train, and a brave young man leapt down and helped the older man to safety, just in the nick of time. Everybody cheered, and then the railway police arrive to arrest the crazed man who was now urinating in full view at the end of the platform.

The incident had shaken Jess and had spoiled the good mood she had been in, and she hurried home thankful that she didn't have to do that journey every day.

She reached home just as it was getting dark, and she tapped on Gertrude's door. "I've brought you a book, and I hope you like it." She asked Jess to come in for a cup of tea and, as it was her birthday, a glass of sherry, and she wanted to hear every detail of her lunch. "I had a lovely day Gertrude, but it was all spoiled by some lunatic on the platform." And she proceeded to tell her all about the incident. "Don't fret about it, dear," Gertrude advised her. "The man that was pushed was okay, wasn't he? And isn't it nice that there are still some heroic souls out there?" She was quite right, of course, and Jess went upstairs to her flat feeling much better about the whole event. She knew that before long it would be Christmas and then she'd be with her loved ones again.

Chapter 6

Two days before Christmas Jess woke up to thick fog. She flicked the light switch, but there was still no power, so she would not be able to wash her hair as she had planned. The water was barely tepid, so she just had a cat's lick of a wash and shivered as she hurriedly put on her clothes. Breakfast was a bowl of muesli, and luckily, the milk from the fridge was still fresh. She was longing for a hot drink, but she would have to wait until she got to work so that she could have a cup of tea, but first, she resolved to call in at the delicatessen.

On her way to work, she threw a box of dry cat biscuits through the factory gate and then attempted to cross the road. She could barely see through the fog and was almost knocked down by a cyclist who shouted at her angrily. The deli was a block further than her office, and she hoped Gregor, the proprietor, would still have some oranges left. All imported food was now in short supply and prices were sky-high, but she was in luck. There was one bag left and so she placed it in her basket along with a small box of chocolate truffles, which was her Christmas present to herself.

As she went to the counter to pay, Gregor gave her a broad grin and said, "I've got something that I've put aside for your boy" – stooping down he produced a chocolate orange with a flourish – "Voila! You said he likes oranges, so this is a little gift from me."

"Oh Gregor, how lovely! These are so hard to find." Gregor laughed. "I know, tell me about it!" Jess was touched at his kindness and thanked him profusely before wishing him a happy Christmas. He saw her out of the shop and said, "Have a good Christmas, I know you will, and make sure to look after that boy of yours."

Gregor had known Josh since he was a toddler, and he knew how much Jess missed him. He sighed as he thought of his grandchildren, who he only managed to see for two weeks a year during the summer holidays. Not for the first time, he wondered what sort of future they would have, and he watched Jess quickly stride away until she disappeared into the fog.

Jess hurried to her office, signed in with the porter, and was gratified to see that the power was on again. She made a cup of tea and took it over to her desk and switched on the computer. They were all going to finish an hour earlier today because some people had to travel long distances, and there were so few trains. She was relieved because it would not be totally dark at four o'clock. She would be able to see if anyone was lurking about in the vicinity of the disused factory. She had purchased a pepper spray on her way to the office that morning, and she would keep it handy in her pocket, just in case.

Sipping her hot tea gratefully, she settled down at the computer to transcribe as much data as she could before the power failed again. She noticed with regret how many more people were defaulting on their payments. She guessed, that sadly, quite a lot of them would most probably become

49

homeless after the start of the New Year. How she hated her job, and if she could have bought her freedom, then they wouldn't have seen her for dust.

At lunchtime, a few of her colleagues were going to the pub for a Christmas drink, and they asked Jess if she wanted to join them. Normally she would have to do her shopping, but she had already bought everything in advance and, feeling in a festive mood, happily tagged along. The pub was serving hot food for lunch, and she ordered a lasagne and guessed that it would be the last hot meal she would have before she reached their home in the country.

At four on the dot, all the computers were switched off and everyone dashed for the exit, wishing each other Merry Christmas and safe journeys. Jess reached home without incident this time and knocked on Gertrude's door, but she could hear the radio on inside and knocked again, but louder this time because the old lady was a little deaf. She heard shuffling footsteps approaching and then then the door was opened a crack and Gertrude asked, "Who's that?"

"It's me, Jess. I've got a little Christmas present for you." Gertrude gasped in amazement. "For me?" And opened the door wider and Jess was surprised to see that she was still in her nightclothes and asked with concern, "You're not feeling ill, are you, Gertrude?"

"No, dear, I just couldn't be bothered to get dressed today, it's been that gloomy. I'm afraid I haven't got any tea to offer you, the pot's gone cold now."

"That's alright," Jess said. "I've got to pack anyway." She bent down and fished in her bag and then produced the bag of oranges which she handed to Gertrude, wishing her a happy

Christmas. Gertrude was delighted and cried, "Oranges! Ooh, how lovely. Are they all for me?"

"Yes of course" – Jess smiled – "and I hope you enjoy them."

"I certainly will dear, and you give that gorgeous boy of yours a hug from me." Suddenly she remembered the little gift she had for Josh and cried, "Wait, give this to him with my love. It's only some chocolate, but I know he likes it."

Jess thanked her and then ran upstairs and unpacked her shopping and to her delight found a triangle of Brie that Gregor must have slipped surreptitiously into her bag. He was always so kind to her, and she would make sure to bring him something nice back from the farm. She began to carefully pack her shopping trolley, wrapping the precious bottles of Brandy and Claret in her sweaters, and on the very top, she put a large bag of dry cat food. She hoped it would be enough and that the poor creatures would be able to survive until her return.

Lastly, she made sure her train ticket was safely in her handbag, and she had wisely bought it well in advance. It was now almost time for the play on the radio, and so she unwrapped her supper of a slice of vegetarian quiche and yoghurt. Once she had eaten, she went to bed with the radio, making sure to set her alarm for seven in the morning.

Once Jess had gone, upstairs Gertrude Trent opened her wardrobe and took out the red dress. She stroked the smooth silk and held it up to herself. It was far too small for her now, of course, but she recalled the day she had bought it, and just how it had made her feel.

She had gone to the department store on Oxford Street with her best friend Alice, to try on some evening dresses, and when she had put on the red dress her fiend's jaw had dropped and she had stammered, "Wow Trudy, you look amazing!" The shop girl had smiled and said, "You know you could almost pass for Marilyn Monroe in that dress." And then Trudy had laughed and in a husky voice sang, 'Happy Birthday Mr President', and then they had all collapsed in a fit of giggles. The dress was expensive, a lot more than she had wanted to pay, but Gertrude said, "I'll take it." And she had imagined the look of admiration on George's face when she put it on, but his reaction had not been at all what she expected, and now, remembering that she angrily pushed the dress back in the wardrobe and slammed the door. The memory had upset her, but then she remembered the oranges that Jess had given her, and when she had popped a few segments into her mouth, she felt better.

The morning of Christmas eve was bright and sunny but with a hint of frost in the air and Jess was relieved that the fog of yesterday had dissipated. She tried the electricity, but it had still not come on and so she had to wash in cold water. The government had promised that on Christmas day they would keep the power on all day, so they were presumably saving today's ration to use tomorrow. She dressed quickly, putting on thick woollen tights under her jeans and two sweaters, a roll neck in fine lambswool, and over it a chunky V-neck. Then she ate a bowl of muesli and a yoghurt for breakfast and put on her warmest coat. She grimaced at the state of her greasy hair as she had wanted to look her best for Sam, but pulled on a knitted hat and her woollen scarf, and her shoulder bag securely across her chest.

There was no point in taking her mobile phone as the battery was flat and she had not been able to charge it in time for her trip. She took a paperback book to read on the journey, and then locking the door behind her, she carefully manoeuvred the heavy shopping trolley down the stairs and out into the street.

Jess walked quickly and soon reached the gates of the abandoned factory where some of the cats were already grouped around waiting for her. She opened the bag of dried food and tossed handfuls through the gate, smiling as the cats jostled for the snacks, eating hungrily, and keeping an eye out for anyone brazen enough to try and steal their portion. A tiny black kitten came running towards her, mewing pitifully, and Jess looked around for the mother. It seemed to be on its own, and she wondered if it was one of the black tomcat's offspring. It was just a scrap of a little thing, and it wasn't getting a chance at the food. Jess gave it a few biscuits and it tried to eat, but its tiny teeth could not cope with the hardness, so with sudden inspiration, Jess popped a couple of the cat biscuits into her mouth to soften them and then the little creature wolfed them down and looked up expectantly for more.

The biscuits tasted disgusting, but Jess softened up some more, and when it had finished them she picked it up and spoke soothingly to it. "You're too tiny to live without someone to look after you, so I can't leave you here, can I?" The kitten struggled at first, not used to being handled, but Jess pulled off her hat and wrapped the little animal in the warm wool. She gave it another couple of softened pellets and stroked it gently, and suddenly it began to purr loudly. She tied her scarf into a sling and popped the kitten inside her coat, and there feeling secure in the warmth and dark, it relaxed and

53

fell asleep. Tipping out the remainder of the cat biscuits, Jess quickly made her way onward to catch the train.

She had a good twenty-minute walk to the tube station, and her train left at midday, but she had planned to get there early hoping that she would then be able to get a seat. A group of homeless, ragged men were grouped around the entrance to the tube and for a moment she felt apprehension. Perhaps the man who had mugged her was one of them, but they all seemed fine, just engrossed in keeping the fire going that they had lit in an old brazier. She saw that one of the men was plucking a pigeon, and he gave her a big grin and said, "How do you like my Christmas turkey?"

When Jess reached the station, the platform was already crowded, as everyone had got the same idea to get there early, and all the seats were full. She managed to squeeze into a space by the doors with her trolley and peeped inside her coat to check on the kitten. It was still fast asleep, and she put her trolley in front of her so that no one could crush against her.

The train somehow filled up even more, with people desperate to get to their loved ones for the Christmas holidays, until not another soul could be fitted onboard. She remembered once seeing a documentary about the Indian railways and had been astonished at how many people had climbed onto the roof to ride the train. If the authorities had allowed it, no doubt many people would have tried to do the same today. Eventually, the whistle blew, and the train moved off, but there were many distraught faces left behind on the platform.

The smell of unwashed bodies was unpleasant, and Jess held her book up in front of her nose, but the position was rather uncomfortable, and eventually, she put it back in her bag. A shabby-looking man was wedged up beside her who kept staring at her, and before too long he began to chat and asked, "Are you going home for the holidays?" Jess nodded, not wishing to get into conversation with him, but he persisted, and after a while said, "You keep on looking down your coat, what have you got in there, the crown jewels?" She had been constantly checking on the little creature, but she gave him a sharp look and retorted, "Sorry to disappoint you, but it's a kitten."

"Is it a Christmas present?"

"Yes, it's for my son." It was a two-hour journey with one stop on the way, and then she would have to change trains and travel for another half hour until she reached her final destination. She hoped he would shut up and not keep on talking to her as his breath smelt foul, but eventually, he was bored with her, and, turning his back, he began to chat to someone else.

At Reading, quite a few people got off, including the nosy man, and she managed to bag a seat before the next lot of passengers squeezed on. At last, she reached Swindon, and there she had to change platforms and wait fifteen minutes for her train. A certain number of vintage steam trains had been resurrected, as some of the coal mines had re-opened in the hunger for fuel, and Jess heard the chuffing of the antique engine with pleasure. It pulled into the station in a cloud of steam, and to her it almost seemed like a living, breathing creature. She climbed aboard quickly and managed to get a seat by the window, and then she checked on the kitten once more. It was still asleep, its tiny chest moving rhythmically up and down, and so she relaxed and watched the panorama of the beautiful frosty countryside unfold before her eyes.

As soon as she reached her destination, she saw to her delight that Josh was running up the platform to greet her, shouting, "Mum, Mum, I've missed you so much!"

"Me too" – she laughed, and then – "Be careful, don't crush my surprise," as he flung his arms around her. She opened her coat and took out the kitten, who sleepily opened his eyes and yawned widely, showing a little pink tongue and tiny needle-sharp teeth.

"Oh, he's so cute!" Josh exclaimed with delight. "What's his name?"

"I thought I'd let you name him," she said, "and it was so lucky that I found him, as he was starving, and he would probably never have survived otherwise."

"Well, in that case, I'll call him Lucky," Josh said, stroking the little kitten gently, which began to purr loudly as if it approved of its name. "Look at you!" Jess exclaimed, gazing with admiration at her son. He had grown into a handsome young man with straight dark hair like her own, but with Sam's blue eyes and winning smile, and she said in amazement, "You're nearly as tall as me now, and is that the beginning of a moustache by any chance?"

Josh blushed, "Yeah, I guess."

"So, where's Daddy?" Jess asked, looking around for Sam.

"Oh, he said he had better stay with the car, as there were a couple of dodgy-looking men hanging around, and he was worried they might try to steal the petrol." They walked quickly out of the station, and when they rounded the corner they saw Sam waiting anxiously by the car, but when he caught sight of her he strode over and, taking her in his arms, kissed her and said, "Oh Jess, it's so good to see you, let me look at you."

"Don't Sam, I look so awful, my hair's filthy and I probably smell."

"I don't care, I'm just so glad to have you home safe and sound." They got into the car and Jess asked Sam how he'd managed to get hold of enough petrol. "I've been saving my ration as I guessed you'd have heavy stuff to carry, and we'd need transport. You must be exhausted after your journey, was it crowded?"

"I'll say!" Jess blew out her cheeks. "All I was dreaming about on the way was a nice hot bath! You do have hot water at home, don't you?"

"Don't worry, there's plenty" – Sam assured her – "and the house is clean and warm, so all you need to do is put your feet up." Jess started to relax, but after a few minutes she asked, "Have you got a Christmas tree yet?"

"Of course, and plenty of holly and ivy, and Josh even made a wreath for the door."

"Oh Sam, it's so good to be home," she told him. "I can't tell you how much I've longed to be here with you both." Sam put a comforting hand on her knee and said, "I know love, but just enjoy every minute and don't think about anything else."

At last, they reached the cottage, and as Jess got out of the car, their dog came bounding over, almost knocking her down in his enthusiasm. "Buster get down! Good boy." She laughed, and he was so excited to see her that he was running in circles around her and barking his deep bark. He was a Rottweiler that Sam had bought two years ago after he had caught a couple of men trying to break into the shed. Whenever he had to leave the cottage empty, he would let

Buster out to roam the grounds as a deterrent to any prospective thieves, and so far, he had done his job very well. They entered the cottage and Jess sniffed the air and asked, "Mm, what is that lovely smell?"

"It's venison stew," Sam replied.

"Where on earth did you manage to find venison?" Jess asked him in surprise.

"Well, it was an accident really," Sam confessed. "I was out shooting rabbits with Johnny Carter in his van, and we knocked down a deer. The poor thing had a broken leg, so we put it out of its misery and shared the bounty." Josh entered the kitchen and put the kitten down on the floor, and immediately a small puddle appeared. Buster came sniffing at the little creature, but it put up a brave paw and batted him on the nose. "Feisty little chap, isn't he?" Laughed Sam. "We'd better find him something to eat."

"I'll warm up some milk, shall I?" Asked Josh, and Jess said, "What can we give him? He's not properly weaned yet." They decide to soak a bit of bread in the milk and then Sam cut up a small piece of ham and mixed that in with it. Josh put down the saucer of warm milk, but the kitten didn't seem to know what to do. "Dip your finger in, Josh, and let him lick it," Sam suggested, and then the kitten suddenly realised what was in the saucer and, dipping in his paw, began to lick it clean of the milk.

Just then, Mrs Purrkins, their older cat squeezed in through the cat-flap and stalked over to them, looking with disdain at the kitten, and then proceeded to lap up all its milk. The little creature watched her from a safe distance, and when Josh re-filled the saucer it attempted to copy the adult cat but managed in the process to get most of the milk all over its whiskers. They watched with amusement as Mrs Purrkins put a firm paw on the kitten's neck and then washed off every trace of milk. "Well, they seem to have bonded" – Jess smiled – "and now, if you don't mind, I'd love to have a bath and wash my hair."

"Shall I bring you a cup of tea?" Asked Sam, and Jess nodded, "That would be heavenly!" She went upstairs and ran the hot water into the bath and then lit the candles, as it was beginning to get dark. Sam had thoughtfully put a clean pair of pyjamas on the bed, and her warm dressing-gown was hanging behind the door. She quickly stripped off her clothes and dropped them into the dirty laundry basket. There was a tiny bit of scented oil left in the bottle, and she poured a few drops into the water and then lowered herself in. It was utter bliss! She could feel all the day's tension gradually ebb from her body as she lay back in the hot water, and she was almost asleep when Sam brought her a mug of tea.

"Would Madam like me to scrub her back?" He asked her in a mock posh accent, and Jess giggled. "If it's not too much trouble, my good man!" He began to gently soap her back and then brought his hands around to her breasts and she sighed contentedly, "Oh, I've missed your touch, why don't you get in with me?" He grinned and was just about to take off his clothes when there was a loud knocking at the door. "Shall I answer it, Dad?" Josh called up the stairs, but Sam said, "No son, go and wait in the lounge, I'm coming down."

It was not safe to open the door to anyone these days, especially as they were so isolated and situated on the very edge of the village, and Sam peered through the window to see who was knocking. It was a shabby-looking old man with a knackered bicycle who was selling firewood, and Sam had half a mind to send him packing, but it was Christmas Eve, and the man looked worn out, so he asked, "How much do you want for the wood?" and the man replied, "Whatever you can spare, Guv'nor." Sam asked hopefully, "Would a ten-pound note do you?"

"Aye, that'll be fine," the man replied, and Sam, feeling benevolent and full of Christmas spirit, said, "Look, why don't you come on in? I've just made a pot of tea and I expect you could do with a cup."

"That's very good of you, Sir," the old man replied, and following Sam into the kitchen, took off his cap and sat down wearily in the chair that was nearest to the Aga. It heated the place very efficiently and kept them with a constant supply of hot water, and the old man would have given anything to own one like it. He looked around and said admiringly, "Nice place you've got here. Have you been here long?"

"About three years. It was my father's place before that. Where are you from?" Sam asked curiously, "I seem to detect a northern accent." The old man nodded, "Aye, I'm from Cumbria. We had a little farm, a bit like this one, but we just kept on getting flooded. In the end, we bought a second-hand motor home and just kept driving till we found a place that would let us stay." Sam asked him, "So where are you based now?"

"T'other side of the village, on farmer Johnson's land. There's about five of us with caravans camped out there, but I don't know how long he will let us stay." Sam handed him a steaming mug of tea and asked, "Would you like a mince pie? They're home-made by my son."

"Aye, thank you very much," the old man said gratefully and proceeded to devour it in two bites. "Have another," Sam offered and then wrapped up another half dozen in some tinfoil. The old man drained his mug and got up to go and Sam gave him the package saying, "You can take these mince-pies home for your wife."

"God bless you, Sir." The old man was touched as he was not used to kindness, as most people sent him off with a mouthful of abuse, so they wished each other Merry Christmas, and Sam watched him ride away and then went to shut up the hens and goats for the night. The hens were already perched in their roosts and Sam locked the door and then went to see the goats. They were warm and snug and had nestled down in the straw in the shed, and he put down fresh water and feed and made sure that they too were locked up securely.

Chapter 7

It was starting to snow as he walked back to the house, and when he went into the living room Jess was kneeling on the floor drying her hair in front of the stove. "Here, let me do that for you," Sam said, squatting down on the rug beside her, and Jess handed him the brush and he lovingly brushed her dark hair smooth over her shoulders. "You smell so good," he murmured, nuzzling her neck, and she smiled and said, "I've been dreaming about this moment for ages." Their reverie was broken when Josh suddenly poked his head around the door and said impatiently, "I'm really, really hungry, Dad, can we eat now?"

"Yes, okay then, I'll just heat some bread," Sam replied. It had spoilt the mood somewhat, so he told Josh to lay the table, and meanwhile, Jess began to unpack her trolley and lay the presents out under the tree. She took the brie and the two bottles of good claret into the kitchen and asked, "Shall we open one of these now, or do you think we should save them both for Christmas Day?"

"Well, there's no time like the present" – Sam grinned – "and I'm sure that red wine will taste just great with the venison."

They sat down at the kitchen table to feast on the delicious venison stew and hot garlic bread and washed it down with a glass of the excellent claret. For dessert, Jess and Sam ate a little of the brie that Gregor had so thoughtfully tucked into her bag, but Josh decided he would rather have one of the oranges that his mother had brought him. "Mm, they're so sweet," he said delightedly, licking the juice from his fingers. "I've been dying to get some of these."

After their meal, Jess did the washing-up and Sam fetched in another load of logs, and then Mrs Purrkins appeared through the cat-flap and shook the snow from her paws. "That reminds me, Josh," Sam said, "you'll need to fill one of the seed trays with earth so that Lucky has somewhere to do his business." The boy had made a bed for the kitten out of one of his old sweaters folded into a shoebox and had placed it next to the Aga, and the little creature was curled up fast asleep.

They took the rest of the wine into the living room and Josh began to tell Jess all the things that he'd been up to over the last few months. "Did you know that we've got two goats now, Mum?"

"Yes" – Jess smiled – "Daddy did mention them to me, the last time we spoke."

"Well, I'm in sole charge of milking them," he told her proudly, "because they don't get on with Dad."

"I'm afraid it's true" – Sam smiled ruefully – "I obviously don't have the right touch."

"Oh, I don't know," Jess said archly, "you've never heard me complain!"

"How gross!" exclaimed Josh in disgust, raising his eyes heavenwards.

"Just you wait till you have a girlfriend," Sam told him, but Josh shook his head and said, "Yuk, I'm never going to go out with a girl."

"I think you will one day" – his father smiled – "it's just that your hormones just haven't kicked in yet." About nine-thirty Josh was beginning to yawn and Sam told him to go up to bed, but Josh protested, "Oh Dad, do I have to go yet?"

"Yes," Sam said firmly, "and the sooner you go to sleep, the sooner it will be Christmas Day, and besides, your mum and I have a lot of catching up to do." Josh got up reluctantly, dragging his feet, and kissed Jess goodnight, then said, "I'm so glad that you're home, Mum, and I wish that you never had to go back."

"Me too, Darling," she said ruefully, trying hard to keep the tears in her eyes from spilling over. When he had gone upstairs Buster whined at the door to be let out, and then Sam came back and sat down on the rug next to her. "Do you want to go up to bed yet?" He asked, but she shook her head. "No, it's so nice and warm here, let's just lie down in front of the fire." Sam kissed her, and she pulled him closer and said, "I've missed you so much. I'd think about you every night before I went to sleep and then wonder if you were doing the same."

"You bet your life! I've been counting the days," Sam told her, then began to kiss her passionately and caress her in all the places that he knew would turn her on. Soon, he was making love to her hungrily and she responded with equal fervour, until at last, all their passion was satisfied. They lay exhausted side by side on the rug, and then Sam, with typical humour, grinned and said, "Well, I suppose we'd better get dressed and go to bed!"

As they filled their hot water bottles, Buster suddenly began to bark and Sam, looking out of the window, saw two shadowy figures running toward the henhouse. "We've got visitors," he told Jess, and then went to unlock the cabinet where he kept his shotgun.

"Is it the man who was here earlier?" Jess asked.

"No, it's a couple of lads I think, but this'll certainly give them a scare," he said, brandishing the shotgun.

"Please be careful," Jess begged, but he reassured her, saying, "Don't worry, it'll be fine."

Buster was circling the two young men, growling, and barking aggressively, and as Sam approached they begged, "Call off your dog please, Mister. We only wanted a few eggs." Buster certainly looked fierce, but he was a sweet-natured dog and wouldn't have attacked them, but the lads were not to know that. They were about eighteen or twenty years old, and Sam could not help noticing that they looked thin and ill-nourished and that one of them was holding a pair of bolt cutters. "Why didn't you knock at the door and buy some then?" Sam demanded, and one of them replied, "We haven't got any money."

"So, you thought it would be okay to steal mine, did you?" Sam said sternly.

"No, but we're desperate, we haven't got anything to eat." The boys looked shamefacedly at the ground, then entreated Sam, "You won't call the police, will you?"

"That depends," Sam said. "If you give me those bolt cutters, we'll say no more about it."

As they handed them over Sam asked, "When did you last eat?" They looked at each other and then one of them replied, "A couple of days ago."

"Well, you'd best come in then. I've got a bit of stew leftover and you're welcome to that." They went nervously ahead of him with Buster following close on their heels, and Sam asked them to sit down at the table. Propping the shotgun well out of their reach, he ladled out two bowls of still warm stew and divided the remainder of the bread between them. They devoured the food with gusto, and with the bread wiped around the bowl so that not a trace of stew remained.

"Thanks, Mister, that was a right treat," one of the lads told him, then asked hesitantly, "Would it be alright for us to go now?"

"Yes, off you go," Sam told them, and handing them a box of six eggs said, "Merry Christmas, but don't let me see you here again, or I will call the police."

"Thanks, Mister!" They couldn't believe their luck, and Sam watched as they cycled away and then went upstairs where Jess greeted him anxiously, "I heard voices. You didn't ask them in, did you?"

"Yeah," Sam said, "but they were so hungry, and I felt really sorry for them. Life's pretty hard for some of the people here Jess."

"I know that Sam," Jess retorted. "I see quite enough real poverty on the streets of London, but they could have been dangerous, and what if they come back? Josh could be hurt."

"I don't think they'll be back," he reassured her, "and anyway, we've got Buster. He was great, and they were quite terrified, poor kids." It was still snowing as he closed the curtains, and soon all traces of their visitors were obliterated.

Chapter 8

Gertrude sat alone on Christmas Day, leafing through an old photo album and thinking about her son, Peter. She hoped that Jess was enjoying the festive season with her son, and her mind wandered back to the time when she had first introduced George to Peter. They had not taken to each other, although George, to give him his due, had tried hard to get the boy to open up.

"So, what football team do you support then, Peter?" he had asked, but the boy had shrugged and said sullenly, "I don't really like football."

"What do you like then? Cricket? Rugby? Tennis maybe?" And each time Peter had shaken his head but eventually he had reluctantly admitted that he liked dancing. George had laughed and said in a derogative manner, "Dancing's for poofs. I meant what kind of sport do you like?" Peter had shrugged and mumbled, "I suppose swimming's okay."

"Alright then," George said heartily, "we'll have a day out at the lido, would you like that?" Peter had nodded, more to please his mother than because he wanted to go, but it seemed to satisfy George. He had prayed fervently that it would rain, but instead, the day had dawned bright and sunny. Gertrude told him the temperature was expected to be hot and to be sure to pack his sun cream. She had made up a picnic lunch for them, and George had arrived promptly at eleven o'clock in his Jaguar to drive them to the lido.

They had put their towels down on their sun loungers and then went to change into their swimming costumes, and when they returned George was already in the water, and vigorously swimming lengths in the pool. Although Peter was now thirteen years old, he was small for his age and self-conscious of his skinny white body, but George trumpeted loudly, "Come on in, the water's lovely!" And then he felt sure that every eye was looking at him and he wanted to disappear. He stood at the edge, tentatively dipping a toe into the water which still felt rather cold to him, but then George laughed and began to splash him, and so he felt he had no option but to jump in.

He came up gasping, and George said, "See, it's not so bad once you're in." Peter would have liked to disagree but said nothing and began to swim slowly along the edge of the pool. "Race you to the far end," yelled George, so Peter swam faster, but of course George was there well before him. "Come on!" he harangued. "You'll never make the Olympics at that rate." Peter had no intention of becoming a competitive swimmer, he just enjoyed being in the water and going at his own pace, but George would not leave him alone. "You're doing it all wrong," he told him, and then proceeded to show him how it was done, saying, "Just move your arms like this and you'll go much faster."

Eventually, Peter was allowed to get out of the pool, and he went to lie in the sun next to his mother as George vigorously towelled himself dry. He then said dismissively to

Gertrude, "That boy has no competitive spirit at all," but she was quick to defend him and retorted, "He has so! It just depends what it is."

She should have realised how unhappy Peter was with George, and looking through her wedding photos, she realised that there was not one picture of him smiling. With typical teenage behaviour, he had just retreated to his bedroom, and only came downstairs when he was feeling hungry.

George had wanted them to have a big, flashy white wedding, whereas she would have been quite happy with a simple registry-office ceremony. She had gone through all the stress of a formal wedding with her first husband, Roy, but George had wanted to show her off. "You'll look so beautiful as my bride," he had insisted, "and anyway I've already bought you a dress." He had gone to fetch a large cardboard box from the boot of his car and when he opened it, she had gasped. It was a frothy white lace creation, with a wide voluminous skirt and Gertrude had really hated it.

"Well?" George had asked with a big grin on his face. "Don't you just love it? You'll look simply amazing walking down the aisle." He had looked like a dog with two tails, and she had not wanted to hurt his feelings, so she had laughed and said, "My Goodness!" Feigning delight. "It must have cost you a fortune, but I don't want a big, white wedding. Anyway, it's supposed to be unlucky for the groom to see the dress before the wedding day. Can you not take it back?"

"I suppose so," he had replied grudgingly, "but I reckon you'd better come with me and choose the one you want, but make sure you pick something expensive, as nothing's too good for my Gertie." Peter had agreed to give her away, but he had firmly drawn the line at making a speech. "I won't know what to say, Mum, all I want is for you to be happy."

She gently ran her finger over his photo and wished she could see him one last time. He looked so like Roy Adams, her first husband, and she wondered what her life would have been like now if he had survived the car crash. She had loved him so much, and he had been a good husband and a hard worker, but when he died, she had found it very hard bringing up a ten-year-old boy on her own. Then, when she met George Bellman three years later, she was ready for another relationship, and he had swept her off her feet.

She had been in a club for a drink with Alice, and it had been the first time she had been out for ages, and when George had walked in heads had turned, but he had made a beeline for Gertrude. He was well over six feet tall, dark, and handsome in a rugged sort of way, and he had such an air of self-confidence, but also of slight menace, that gave one the impression he was not a man to be messed with.

"Can I buy you lovely ladies a drink?" He had asked, and without waiting for a reply had ordered the barman to give them the same again, ordering a double scotch for himself. He had flashed a dazzling smile at Gertrude and asked her name. "Gertrude," she had replied, "but my friends call me Trudy or Trude."

"Well, I don't like the sound of Trude, it sounds like a prude, so I'm going to call you Gertie," George had said. She had always hated being called Gertie, but how could she argue with such a handsome man, especially when he called her Gorgeous Gertie? "Are you married?" he had asked, and she told him she was a widow and had a 13-year-old son. He had asked her out to dinner the following day, Alice had agreed to babysit, and he had taken her to a smart casino where everybody seemed to know him. She had felt a little self-conscious, as she only had one decent cocktail dress, and she felt sure that it must look a little dated in comparison to what the other women were wearing.

It seemed that George had thought so too, because he had asked her what she was doing the following day, and when she had replied, "Nothing much," he had said. "In that case, I'm taking you shopping. You're going to need a few smart outfits if you're going out with me. Meet me outside Selfridges at eleven o'clock tomorrow morning." As the taxi stopped outside her house, he had kissed her goodnight and grinned. "Don't keep me waiting!"

Gertrude didn't know what to think. George must be wealthy, but she hardly knew him and so how could she consider letting him buy her clothes? On the other hand, he wanted to feel proud of her and she didn't have the money to spend on new outfits, so she asked her friend, Alice, what she should do.

"Do you like him?" Her friend had asked her, and when she said that she did, Alice had replied, "Well then, don't look a gift horse in the mouth. Let him buy you what he wants and just be happy about it." She had her doubts about George, but she didn't voice them to Gertrude because she was so obviously smitten, but she wouldn't have touched him with a barge pole. He was certainly good-looking and had presence, but he also had an air of latent aggression, and she could just imagine that he could turn very nasty if he didn't get what he wanted.

Gertrude arrived at Selfridges at five to eleven and George had appeared at eleven on the dot. "Good girl, bang on time," he had said, kissing her on the cheek. "Now, let's go and choose a few nice frocks for you." Gertrude was in a dream as he led the way to the women's wear department, and he quickly picked out half a dozen dresses for her to try on. "Come and show me," he had commanded, and then it was either a yes, or a no, and soon he had chosen two cocktail dresses and two ball gowns, only one of which she would have picked for herself. "Now we need to buy you a nice outfit and a hat for Ascot next week," he told her. After some deliberation, he bought her a floral silk dress and jacket and a rather silly hat that Gertrude would not have chosen in a month of Sundays. She would just have to grin and bear it and try to look sophisticated and not show herself up in front of his rich friends.

George bought her lunch and then said he had some business to attend to and slipped her £20 for a taxi to take her home. "I'll pick you up next Saturday night at seven as I'm taking you to a dinner dance at a swish country hotel, and I thought perhaps we could stay the night." He had just assumed that she would be free, which of course she was, but he had forgotten about Peter. "I'll have to see if I can get a babysitter," she told him firmly, and then he frowned and asked, "How old is your boy?"

"He's thirteen."

"Then surely he's quite old enough to look after himself." Gertrude thought otherwise but said, "Alright then, I'll phone Alice and see if she's free."

"Okay, I'll pick you up at seven o'clock sharp." It was an order, not a question, and she hoped that her friend had not made other plans.

Alice had indeed made plans to go out with a few girlfriends, but she said that Peter could stay over. Instead of going out she would invite the girls over for a pamper party, and she would get in some wine and nibbles. "I hope you've got some sexy underwear, Trudy," she told Gertrude with a grin, "We don't want him to be put off by all the holes in your pants."

"Cheek!" laughed Gertrude. "They're not that bad," but then she had to agree that her underwear was not designed to inflame a man's passions. It now involved another shopping trip, and she invested in two lacy bras with matching panties and a silky nightdress. Alice nodded her approval and said, "If those don't get him going, nothing will!"

Saturday afternoon, Gertrude had her hair done and delivered Peter over to Alice's flat. He was rather looking forward to the evening and asked Alice, hopefully, if any of her friends would let him do their hair. "I'm sure they would," she told him, "and if they won't, you can always do mine." Peter wanted to be either a hairdresser or a graphic designer, he hadn't yet decided which, but he was artistic. He enjoyed the company and banter of women, and Gertrude wondered if perhaps he might be gay. He was certainly sensitive and was not at all interested in the usual masculine pursuits.

At the hotel, George ordered a scotch on the rocks and a cocktail for Gertrude, and over their drinks, she asked him if he'd ever been married. "Yeah, twice," he replied, and she asked curiously, "What happened, did you divorce them?"

"The first wife, I did. She was always moaning, and a real nagging cow. If it's one thing in a woman I can't stand, it's nagging." Gertrude made a mental note never to nag, and then asked, "What about your second wife?"

"She died," he said abruptly.

"Oh, I'm so sorry. Do you still miss her?"

"No, not at all," George replied, and at Gertrude's surprised look he added, "We weren't suited. I'm sorry she had to die, but I don't miss her at all." His mouth set in a hard line, and he took a slug of whisky, and she thought it would probably be wise not to ask any more questions, although she was curious about the circumstances of her death, so to change the subject she asked, "What kind of music do you like?"

"Mainly tunes from the shows, something that I can sing along to," George had replied, but Gertrude had then laughed delightedly and said, "I just can't imagine you singing."

"What do you mean you cheeky minx?" George said indignantly. "I've got a fine voice, and you can hear me sing in the shower tonight if you play your cards right."

"Now who's being cheeky?" Gertrude said, a smile dimpling her cheeks. George then took her hand and began to gently stroke the inside of her arm up to the elbow, never taking his eyes off her face, and she felt a delicious thrill under his unrelenting gaze and the touch of his fingers. After a minute or two he grinned broadly and said, "Oh yes, I think you really, really do want to hear me sing in the shower." She blushed and thought to herself, *"He's a man who knows how to get exactly what he wants,"* and she had to admit that she rather liked it.

They ended up in a room in the hotel, and the next morning, once she was back home, she couldn't wait to phone Alice to tell her all about the evening and confessed, "Guess what, I slept with George last night."

"Well, and how was it?" Alice asked curiously.

"Amazing, the best sex I've ever had. I came twice!"

"You lucky thing!" Alice said enviously. "I'd hold on to him if I were you, as there aren't that many good men around."

"I don't know if he's good," Gertrude mused. "I think he's a bit of a bad boy actually, but I can't help liking him."

George had proposed to her six weeks later, but it was far from romantic. He had called to pick her up to go to the races, but he was a little early, and Gertrude was not ready. While he waited, she made him a coffee and left him to wander around the small, walled garden, inspecting the flowering shrubs while she went upstairs to get dressed.

She had opted for a French navy lace dress and matching jacket topped with a small feather fascinator, and George had smiled his approval. "You look lovely," he said, pleased that she had chosen one of the outfits he had bought for her. "You've got a very nice garden here, but it's a bit on the small side," he told her. "Mine's about six times the size."

"We didn't need a big garden," Gertrude said, "as Roy and I were both members of Kew Gardens, we'd get free entry as often as we liked." Their house was in a quiet, tree-lined street, only about a fifteen-minute walk from the gardens, and they had often taken a picnic and spent the afternoon with Peter playing happily with a ball or a frisbee.

"These houses must be worth quite a bit, I should think," George said in an offhanded manner and Gertrude had to agree. "Yes, last year, there was one down the road that sold for well over a million."

"Amazing, isn't it?" He sniffed. "Especially as it hasn't even got a garage." The house had a small, paved parking area in the front, but George's large Jaguar wouldn't fit into the space, and he'd had to drive around the block a couple of times to try and find somewhere to park. "Of course," he said, "once we're married, we'll be living in my house."

Gertrude gasped and swung around in surprise. "What did you say?"

"I said once we're married…"

"George! Was that a proposal by any chance?"

"I suppose it was," he laughed. "I meant to ask you before, so what's it to be?"

"I'll have to consider it," she replied, taken completely by surprise.

"What's to consider?" He grinned. "I love you and you love me, don't you?" She nodded, and then he said, "Well then, let's get married!"

"I want to talk to Peter first," she said firmly, "and I'll let you know tomorrow." George wasn't used to being made to wait, but he could see that she needed to talk things over with her son. He decided he would be patient a little while longer, although he was quite convinced the answer would be yes.

Gertrude was not quite so sure. George could be rather bombastic at times, whereas Roy had been quiet and gentle, and they had always talked things over. George was used to getting his way, but he was generous and good company and amazing in bed, and just thinking about it gave her a little frisson of excitement. She phoned Alice and told her that George had asked her to marry him, but she wasn't sure if she should. "What's giving you doubts, Trudy?" Alice asked her. "I thought you were mad about him."

"Well, I don't know how Peter will take it. George is so different to how Roy was."

"Peter's a big boy now, and he'll be leaving school in a couple of years and going to college, so don't lose your chance of happiness because he might not approve. He does make you happy, doesn't he?" She asked with concern.

"Most of the time" – Gertrude laughed – "but he does like to get his way."

"What man doesn't!" Alice retorted, and Gertrude decided if Peter wasn't too unhappy about it, then she would go ahead and accept George's proposal.

That afternoon, when Peter came home from school, she asked, "Darling, what do you think of George?" Peter shrugged nonchalantly and replied, "He's alright I suppose."

"So how would you feel if we got married, would you be upset?"

"I don't think he's a patch on Dad, but if you love him, Mum, then go for it."

Gertrude had laughed delightedly and ruffled his hair, saying, "My word, you've become such a grown-up young man now, and you are your father's son."

She was going to call George the next day, but he phoned first and with typical impatience asked, "So what's your answer Gertie, is it yes?"

"Yes George, I will marry you."

"Good! I'll take you out for lunch and we can discuss when and where, and you'll need a new dress." He had bought Gertrude a stunning and very expensive diamond engagement ring, and he had presented it to her during lunch. She had gasped at the size of the diamond, but if she had known where the money to purchase it had come from, she would have thrown it right back in his face.

The wedding had been a quiet, registry office affair just as she had wanted, with just a few of their closest friends invited, and not the big white wedding with all the bells and whistles that George had planned, but the honeymoon had more than made up for it.

Suddenly, the phone rang, shocking Gertrude out of her reverie, and it was her dear friend, Alice. "I just wanted to wish you a Merry Christmas," she wheezed, and Gertrude said with concern, "You sound awful. Are you not any better?"

"No. I just can't seem to shake off this damn chest infection. I've been in bed all day."

"Well just make sure you go and see the doctor as soon as the surgery's open," Gertrude urged her, "and don't let them fob you off."

She was worried sick about her friend, and her worst fears were confirmed a few days later when she had a call from Alice's niece.

"I'm so sorry to have to tell you, but Aunt Alice went into the hospital with pneumonia yesterday, and I'm afraid she died."

Gertrude was very shaken, and suddenly felt quite faint and had to sit down. "Oh Alice, whatever will I do without you," she said aloud, and then began to cry, the tears running down her cheeks unchecked. She couldn't believe that she would never see her dearest and only friend again, and with her son, Peter missing somewhere in Australia, she suddenly came to realise the awful truth that she was now totally alone in the world.

Chapter 9

Christmas Day dawned bright and cold, and Jess woke up to the sun streaming in through the window, and she stretched luxuriously in the comfortable double bed. There was a tap on the door and Josh came in bringing her a cup of tea and said, "Dad said to tell you breakfast will be ready in twenty minutes, and how do you want your eggs?"

"Oh, I think scrambled please, and Merry Christmas Josh!"

"Yeah, Merry Christmas, Mum. I can't wait to open my presents."

"Well, you'll have to wait, as nothing is to be opened till after breakfast." It had always been a family rule to wait, to make the anticipation last a little longer, and it had taught Josh a valuable lesson in discipline. She got up and showered, luxuriating in the feel of hot water on her skin, then quickly towelled herself dry and dressed in a warm pair of slacks and a soft pink angora sweater that she had come across in a charity shop. She brushed her hair and put on a bit of lipstick and then she was ready to go down to breakfast.

The smell of the food cooking was making her juices flow. As she entered the warm and cosy kitchen, Sam was just in the process of plating up the eggs. "Mm, that smells great," she told him, "and I'm really hungry."

"So am I" – he grinned – "especially as I've already fed all the animals and collected the eggs, and Josh has milked and mucked out the goats."

"Then you both deserve the rest of the day off, so I'll cook the dinner while you two just relax and enjoy yourselves."

After they had eaten, Jess did the washing up while Josh dried, and Sam fetched in a load more logs for the fire, and then they all went into the living room to open their presents. The Christmas tree had been nicely decorated by Josh, who had painted some fir cones gold and silver and hung coloured ribbons and cut-out figures of angels from its branches, but Jess missed the magical glow of the fairy lights. She remembered, sadly, how Christmas had always been such a festival of lights, with each town trying to outdo the show of the year before, and how the big department stores would dream up new and magical displays for their windows. People used to come from across the world to see the lights in Oxford Street and Regent Street, and she had loved to see what Liberty's and Selfridges would come up with each year, as they would always present something extra special. Now, without lights, Christmas displays were not a patch on what they used to be, but then there were very few foreign visitors, and people didn't have the money to spend anyway.

Here, in the countryside, it was a simpler affair, with people bringing in bunches of holly and ivy to decorate their homes, and the lighted candles in people's windows looked warm and welcoming. Josh didn't remember the lights of London, as he had been only three or four when the ban on non-essential lighting had been introduced. He was a real country boy now and was delighted with Sam's gift of a warm and waterproof jacket, as he was fast growing out of his old one, with the sleeves ending halfway up his wrists. However, it was Jess's present of the compendium of games that thrilled him. "Thanks, Mum, that's brilliant! Now Dad and I will never be bored again of an evening!" The gift of oranges also pleased him, but it was Gregor's gift of a chocolate orange that had intrigued him. He had never seen one before and begged to be allowed to try some.

"Alright, just a couple of segments," Jess told him, "or you'll spoil your appetite."

"There's no chance of that." Sam grinned. "He's eating me out of house and home at the moment." Jessica insisted that Sam open his gifts next, and he was thrilled with the book. "That's just what I was looking for, it's going to be invaluable. Where on earth did you find it?"

"It was just a lucky fluke," smiled Jess, and the bottle of brandy brought a big grin to his face, and he told her, "You sure know the way to spoil a guy, and with the help of the book, we could be drinking our wine next year." Josh had saved up his pocket money to buy his father a new pair of gloves, but he couldn't wait for Jess to open his present to her. It was a simple, polished wooden box with a small lock and key. It was beautifully made, with dovetailed corners, and inside was a velvet cushion, and the lid was carved with three birds in flight.

"I made that especially for you in woodwork," he told her proudly, "and the birds are meant to be a representation of us flying home from the city to safety here."

"Darling, that's beautiful," Jess told him, her eyes brimming with unshed tears. "You are so clever and thoughtful, and I'll always treasure it."

"It's to put your treasures in," he told her earnestly, and Sam smiled and said, "I think this might fit the bill," handing her a small leather box. Inside was a pair of diamond and pearl earrings, and Jess gasped. "They're beautiful, but they must have cost you a fortune!"

"No," Sam shrugged, "they were quite reasonable actually. I was lucky and found them at a local auction where most people were only looking for farming implements." Jess put them on and went to admire them in the mirror but thought sadly that she would probably never go anywhere smart enough to wear them. He had also given her a bright, striped knitted scarf decorated with pompoms at each end, and he told her it had been made by the lady in the post office. It was warm and cosy, and she would be certain to wear that.

Jess began to prepare the vegetables for their Christmas dinner while Sam showed Josh the rules of chess. The day before, he had bought a goose from a local farmer with the proviso that it was plucked and ready for the oven. The giblets were to be a treat for Buster, but Jess was not used to the Aga. She had to ask Sam how long the bird needed in the oven, and when she went into the living room, he and Josh were both sprawled on the rug in front of the fire engrossed in a game of chess.

Eventually, all was ready, and then she lit the candles and called them into the kitchen. She had dressed the worn pine kitchen table with a red tablecloth and sprigs of ivy, and there were festive napkins and their best crystal glasses. The good bottle of claret had already been decanted, and Sam began to carve the goose while Jess served up the roasted vegetables.

Suddenly, the cloth began to move, and Jess had to hold it fast to prevent everything from sliding to the floor. It was Lucky, the kitten, who was hanging on for dear life and trying his best to climb up to where the delicious smell was coming from. Josh scooped him up and held him on his lap and fed him titbits of goose, but Sam frowned and said, "You'll spoil that cat, but I'll let it pass just this once as it's Christmas Day." The Christmas pudding was delicious and had been made by one of the ladies in the village, and Jess poured a little of the precious brandy over it and lit it to Josh's delight. She served it up with double cream, and Josh let Lucky lick the spoon under the table when Sam wasn't looking.

After they had eaten until they were full to bursting, they retired to the other room where Sam and Josh resumed their chess game and Jessica got out the book she had bought for the train journey and read until the light began to fade. It was time to shut in the hens and goats, and Sam took Buster out for his daily walk while Jess tackled the washing-up and Josh helped with the drying up.

No one could eat very much for supper, so Jess prepared a few hams and homemade pickle sandwiches, and then they played Rummy until Josh began to yawn and said he was off to bed. "Do you want to go up yet?" Sam asked, but Jess sighed contentedly and said, "No, let's just cuddle up here in front of the fire for a while. It's been such a perfect day, and I've been dreaming about this for ages. If only it could always be like this."

"That's my dream too" – Sam sighed – "and one day, Darling, I'm sure it will be, but for now we'll just have to make the most of the time we have together."

Later, as they were getting ready for bed, Jesse's thoughts turned to Gertrude. She hadn't been looking at all well lately, and she hoped the old lady had not had to spend the day alone, and that her friend, Alice, had been able to visit her. She had often wondered what had made Gertrude so afraid to leave the house, but every time Jess had tried to ask her about it, she had quickly changed the subject, so it became quite obvious that she didn't want to talk about the reason for her fear.

Chapter 10

Once Gertrude had got over the shock of Alice's death, she made herself a strong cup of tea and put in a good slug of whisky. Her photo album had fallen on the floor, and as she picked it up, a picture fell out, of her and George on their honeymoon. It was taken in Rome, by the famous fountain, and she had heard that if she threw in a coin and made a wish it would come true, and one day she would return to Rome. She couldn't remember what she had wished for, but whatever it was it hadn't come true, and neither had she returned to Rome. If she had known then how her life would end up, she would have run a mile. In a fit of anger, she picked up a biro and scribbled all over George's smug face.

She had felt so happy and excited when George had told her he was taking her on a three-week cruise around the Mediterranean Sea for their honeymoon. Alice had very kindly agreed to let Peter stay with her for the duration, and the boy had loved spending some time alone with her, without the stress of having George on his back all the time.

The honeymoon was wonderful at first, but it was not to last. The first little cloud on the horizon happened while they were in Rome. They had been to see all the usual tourist sights, the Colosseum, the Spanish Steps, and the beautiful marble sculptures of the Trevi Fountain, where a charming old man had told her in halting English to throw in a coin and make a wish. It would come true, providing that she never told it, and one day she would return to the eternal city. George had simply laughed and said, "You are so gullible Gertie, you don't believe in all that rubbish, do you?"

"Yes, I do, and it's not rubbish," Gertrude had protested, and she had thrown in a one-euro coin and wished sincerely that George and Peter would become the best of friends. Afterwards, they had lunch at one of the little open-air cafes in the square, but then a drunken man, who reeked to high heaven, came begging around the tables and annoying everyone until eventually one of the waiters had chased him away.

A few moments later another beggar came to their table and entreated them to give alms, but this time it was a bent, aged lady dressed in a ragged black dress. Gertrude immediately got out her purse, but George swore and angrily drove her away. Feeling pity for the old woman, Gertrude got up and ran after her and thrust a ten euro note into her gnarled old hand. "Grazzi Senora," the old woman said gratefully, and before she could stop her, she had grabbed Gertrude's hand and kissed it. George simply looked at her with disdain and said, "You didn't fall for that act, did you? She's probably laughing all the way to the bank."

"I don't know how you can be so heartless, George. Didn't you notice her hands? They were crippled with arthritis, so she wouldn't be able to work, and maybe she has no one to care for her." George shrugged and said, "More fool you for falling for a typical scam. She's probably got her sons waiting around the corner rubbing their hands in glee." It left a sour note to the day and Gertrude began to wonder if she knew him at all.

The next day was the evening of the Captain's Ball, and Gertrude had been looking forward to it. She had splashed out on a beautiful red silk evening gown that showed off her ample cleavage and trim figure perfectly, and to set it off, she had put on a pair of long sparkly earrings. She admired her reflection in the mirror, turning this way and that, and she felt a million dollars, and so when George came out of the bathroom, she had expected to be complimented on her looks, but instead, he looked her up and down and said, "What on earth are you wearing? You look just like a cheap tart."

Gertrude's eyes stung with tears, and she protested, "But I bought this dress especially for tonight. It was very expensive, and I think it's really lovely."

"Well, I don't. Either you take it off or you can stay in the cabin for the duration."

Gertrude seethed with anger, but she said nothing and just sighed and removed the dress, and then George went to the wardrobe and pulled out a black lacy dress which had a high boat-neck and elbow-length sleeves and threw it at her, saying, "Here, wear the dress I bought you, at least you'll look a bit more classy." She put it on but thought it was quite frumpy, far more suitable for someone of her mother's age, or even her grandmother. All the pleasurable anticipation of the evening had dissipated, and she followed George meekly to the ballroom. As they danced she could not help but notice that his eyes frequently strayed to the cleavages of some of the more attractive women, and she could have cheerfully throttled him. Instead, she drank too much wine and flirted outrageously with one of the young stewards, hoping to make her husband jealous, but instead, he deliberately ignored her. Later, however, George was furious when he had to ask one of the stewards to help him get her back to the cabin. Needless to say, she had a very sore head in the morning, and her new husband took great delight in pointing out that she had brought it entirely on herself.

When they got back from their honeymoon, George had insisted that they live in his house in Chigwell in Essex, and he had wanted her to sell her family home in Kew. Gertrude had only been to his house a couple of times, and it was not to her taste. It was a large, modern building in a gated courtyard and had been showily decorated with reproduction ormolu furniture and gilt mirrors everywhere. It was not a cosy or comfortable place like hers, but it had been designed solely to make an impression for when he brought people around.

George had wanted Gertrude to open a joint account and to sell her house as soon as possible, but she had always had her own bank account and it gave her a feeling of security, but he had taken offence and asked, "What's the matter, don't you trust me then?"

"Yes, of course, I trust you, but I'm not going to sell my house," she had told him firmly. "I've made a decision and I'm going to rent it out and put the money aside for Peter's future." He said nothing, but inwardly fumed, and his attitude was noticeably cooler towards her and her son, and Peter was understandably upset about having to move to Chigwell.

"I don't want to go, Mum," he had pleaded. "Please can't I stay here to be near my friends?" It was not an option, as he was not old enough to live on his own, so she had to find a school for him in the vicinity. She knew it would probably mean that his schoolwork would suffer, and just when he was beginning to study for his GCSEs, but there was nothing to be done. Gertrude had also tried to find somewhere locally that did the ballet and tap classes that he so enjoyed, but the only ones she could find were for little girls. When she told George, he laughed uproariously and said, "Well it's about time he grew a pair! Ballet and tap, it's not manly, is it?"

"I suppose Nureyev and Fred Astaire weren't manly then?" Gertrude quipped, but George had just shrugged and said, "Well they were an exception."

Gertrude had previously worked in a health-food shop in Richmond, but she'd had to give in her notice and wanted to find something similar in Chigwell, but George wouldn't hear of it.

"I don't want my wife going out to work," he said emphatically. "You don't need the money as I give you everything that you need, and I want you to be here when I get home." It wasn't so much the money that Gertrude would miss, but the companionship and contact with people. She had been used to meeting Alice once a week for a drink or a pizza after work, but that was just not possible anymore.

She had managed to find a tenant very quickly for her house in Kew and had put all her furniture into storage. George had been scathing about her things, and adamant that he didn't want 'all that tat' in his house. She thought that Peter might be glad of it when he eventually moved into his own place. She blessed her first husband for having the foresight to take out some life insurance, as it now meant that the house was mortgage-free, and she had the rent paid directly into her account. After the council tax and heating bills were paid, there was still enough left to set up a trust fund for Peter and a little nest egg for herself.

George was still annoyed with her because she wouldn't open a joint account, but she liked to feel independent and the fact that she had refused had irked him. "In that case," he had told her, "you can damn well pay for your son because I'm not going to give him a single penny." He paid all the household bills, and he told her if she wanted a new pair of shoes for herself, or to get her hair done, then he would happily give her the money, but he stuck to his word about Peter, and would not even provide his dinner money for school.

Gertrude had no real idea what George did for a living. He had once told her he was a commodities broker, buying cheap and selling for a substantial profit, but there was a side of his business she knew nothing about. He often brought people to the house that he called business associates, and they would go into his study and close the door. Once she had attempted to go in, but the door had been locked, and George had opened it a crack and said tersely, "Don't bother me now, Gertie," and quickly shut the door, and then she had heard the key turn in the lock. She had only wanted to ask if they wanted a drink, but the fact that he had to lock her out began to rouse her suspicions.

She hadn't much liked any of the friends George introduced her to. The men were all a bit too brash, and their over-made-up and perma-tanned wives seemed to be interested only in where their next holiday was going to be. She was beginning to think that marrying George had been a mistake, but then he would show his loving and considerate side, and she would forgive him, and without a doubt, she had to admit that he was very good in bed.

George's fortieth birthday was in the middle of August, and Gertrude racked her brains to think of a suitable gift for him. She decided that the perfect present to buy him was a diver's watch, as she knew he liked watches, and it was something that he could wear in the pool when they went on holiday. She phoned Alice to see if she was free for lunch, and then took the tube to the west-end where she managed to find a suitable watch, and she also bought him an expensive T-shirt. It was wonderful to see Alice again, but her friend noticed that everything was not as it should be and asked gently, "What's wrong Trudy?"

"Nothing," Gertrude had replied and then burst into tears. It all came out then, how lonely she was feeling in that big house, and how much the tension between George and her son upset her, and the fact that Peter was deeply unhappy at his new school. "He hasn't made any friends, Alice, he just eats his tea and then goes straight up to his room."

"Do you think he'd like to spend the weekend with me?" Alice asked her. "It might cheer him up and get him out of George's way for a bit."

"Oh Alice, I think he'd love that," Gertrude said gratefully. "You are a true friend!"

When she got home, she wrapped George's presents and began to prepare their evening meal, but George arrived home early in an ebullient mood and said, "Leave all that for now Gertie. I'm going to take you out to have a Chinese meal, and tomorrow you'd better get packing as we're spending my fortieth birthday in Las Vegas!"

"What, do you mean the three of us?"

"No, I'm not taking Peter. It's no place for a boy. It'll be just you and me, and Lenny and Caroline, and I've booked us a week in the Holiday Inn, so what do you say?"

"Wow, Las Vegas!" She said with as much enthusiasm as she could muster, as she was in two minds about the trip. On the one hand, she had always wanted to see the Grand Canyon, but on the other hand, she could not stand George's best friend's wife. Of all the women that George had introduced her to, Caroline was the most empty-headed, with an annoying little giggle that made you want to strangle her after a few minutes in her company. She phoned Alice to see if Peter could stay with her for the week. "You don't even have to ask, he's always welcome here" – her friend assured her – "as long as he doesn't mind being on his own while I'm at work."

Peter was very happy about the arrangement, and it was the first time that Gertrude had seen him smile for ages. "Don't you worry, Mum." He had reassured her. "I'll go and see some of my old friends, and I certainly won't be bored." He had declined to come to the Chinese restaurant with them but had asked Gertrude if she would bring him back a takeaway.

The next day, she was busy packing for the three of them, and she had wanted to accompany Peter to Alice's flat, but he had pooh-poohed the idea and said, "Mum, I'm fourteen now and I'm quite capable of getting there on my own."

"Well, okay," she replied, "but please ring me just as soon as you get there." She knew that she was being over-protective, but he was her only child, and she couldn't bear it if something awful were to happen to him.

Alice was delighted to have Peter stay, and over supper that night she asked him how he was getting along with George. He pulled a face and said, "I hate him."

"Why? He doesn't touch you, does he?" Alice asked with concern, but Peter shook his head and replied, "No, but he's threatened to. He's always on my case."

A couple of weeks previously, George had come home early to find Peter engrossed in doing his homework on the dining room table. They were expecting guests, and Gertrude had gone out to the corner shop to get some wine, so George eyed Peter with annoyance and said, "Get all that crap moved off the table now."

"I haven't finished my homework yet," Peter protested, but George barked, "I don't care, get it shifted now, and be quick about it."

"It'll be your fault if I fail my exams," Peter muttered half under his breath but began slowly to clear away his books.

"Don't you dare give me any lip," George retorted, "or I'll give you a thick ear."

"If you touch me, I'll tell Mum," Peter replied, and George sneered, "Yeah, that's right, run to Mummy, you namby-pamby little poof. Get out of my sight, you make me sick."

Peter took himself upstairs and slammed the door to his bedroom, and when Gertrude went up to fetch him down for dinner, he told her he wasn't hungry. It set the pattern for the future, for if George was at home he would stay in his room, preferring to take his meals there in peace. Now at Alice's place, he could relax and be himself without the ever-critical eye of his stepfather watching his every move.

Chapter 11

Early next morning, their flight left from Heathrow, and while they were waiting, Gertrude chose a couple of paperback books in duty-free to read on the journey. At last, after what seemed like endless hours of flying, she was excited to see the spectacular lights of Las Vegas below them. But the long flight had left them all exhausted, and at the hotel, they went straight to bed.

The next morning, after a very large and satisfying American breakfast which included waffles with maple syrup, George and Lenny were eager to go off to a casino. Their wives decided to accompany them, but after an hour or so on the fruit machines, they were both utterly bored and wanted to leave.

"I'm going back to the hotel to top up my tan by the pool," Caroline said. "Are you coming?"

"Maybe later," Gertrude replied, but first, she was keen to see the sights of Las Vegas. On the way over, she had noticed that there was a bus that did a tourist trip around the city, and it left quite frequently from a stop near their hotel. She bought a ticket and thoroughly enjoyed the tour, marvelling at all the different, outlandish styles of the buildings, and seeing the homes of the famous film stars. She was glad not to have to listen to Caroline's inane chatter in her ear for the duration. When the bus had dropped her off near the hotel, Gertrude went straight up to her room and changed into her swimming costume. The men were still not back from the casino, but Caroline saw her and waved to her from the pool and called, "Over here, Gertie, I've saved you a sunbed."

"I do wish you wouldn't call me Gertie," she said with irritation, "I hate it."

"Well, what shall I call you then?"

"Trudy, or Gertrude."

"Okay, Trudy it is, but then why does George always call you Gertie?"

"I couldn't tell you" – Gertrude shrugged – "I suppose he likes it. Tell me, did you ever get to know his other two wives?" she asked out of interest, as George wasn't at all forthcoming and she would have liked to know a lot more about his past.

"I didn't know his first wife," Caroline replied, "but I knew Gemma quite well."

"What was she like?" Gertrude asked curiously.

"Well, she was very kind and caring, and quite good fun at first," Caroline told her, "but then she kind of went a bit strange."

"How do you mean, in what way strange?"

"She became awfully moody and thought that people were out to get her. I blamed it on the drugs as she was quite a coke-head. It was a such shame really because she was stunningly beautiful, and she was always appearing in magazines like Vogue. Then she started to lose her looks and of course, then she stopped getting the work."

"Did George know about her drug habit?" Gertrude asked, and Caroline gave one of her silly giggles and said, "You are joking, aren't you?"

"What do you mean?"

"Oh dear, I've said far too much already," Caroline said, putting a finger to her lips. "If you want to know more, you'd better ask your husband."

Gertrude felt rather put out, and she wondered why Caroline was being so mysterious, but it was not something she could question George about. However, she had an uneasy feeling that he was mixed up in something rather unsavoury. She began to smooth sun-cream onto her legs and positioned the sunshade so that her face was shielded from the glare of the sun. She then got out the book that she had started to read on the plane.

"What are you reading?" Caroline enquired curiously, and Gertrude replied, "It's a book about the Tudors."

"Oh history, how boring!" Caroline laughed, but Gertrude snapped back, "No one could accuse the Tudors of being boring."

"Well, each to his own." Caroline shrugged and took out her earphones and began to listen to the latest pop music, tapping her fingers annoyingly in time to the beat. After a while, they felt too hot and so took a leisurely dip in the pool to cool off, and then ordered cocktails. Caroline said peevishly, "I think the fellers seem to have forgotten all about us. They must be on a winning streak." However, when they finally turned up as the sun was going down, Gertrude saw from George's face that it had not been a successful day. He was very quiet over dinner, and Lenny was not very talkative either, so Gertrude told them all about her sightseeing tour. Caroline suggested that they hit the shops the next day.

"Don't you go mad with the credit card," Lenny warned her, "as we've got to try and recoup our losses tomorrow."

The next morning, the men headed straight back to the casino, and Caroline, after much cajoling, eventually persuaded Gertrude to go to the shops with her. However, this proved to be a big mistake, as Caroline was a nightmare to shop with, never making her mind up about anything, and by lunchtime, Gertrude decided that she'd had enough.

"I'm going back to the hotel," she told Caroline, who begged her, "Please, let's go and see just one more shop. I want to get a nice present for Lenny." Gertrude sighed and reluctantly agreed, just as long as that was the last one.

"Anyone would think you don't like shopping," Caroline said with astonishment. "I love it. I'd go shopping all day, every day if Lenny would let me." She had bought him a gaudy T-shirt that had palm trees and 'I love Las Vegas' on the front, the word love replaced by a heart. Gertrude thought it was the height of vulgarity but decided to keep her opinion to herself. She had only bought a pretty pair of sandals for Alice and a T-shirt and a Las Vegas pennant for Peter, but Caroline struggled back to the hotel with her arms laden with carrier bags, and she hoped for his sake that Lenny had won plenty of dollars that day.

When the men returned, it seemed that they had completed a successful day's gambling as they were both in a good mood, and as they were changing for dinner George gave Gertrude a small box and said, "Here's a little keepsake of Las Vegas for you Sweetheart." She opened the box to find a pair of eighteen-carat gold earrings in the shape of dollar signs and they were studded all over with diamonds. "Put them on then," George said, and she dutifully obeyed.

"Thank you, George. They're a perfect memento of our holiday," she said, kissing him on the cheek. They were not all to her taste, being much too flashy, but she was amused to see his look of pride when Caroline gushed her approval of them over dinner. "Oh Trudy, they're just fabulous! Are those diamonds real?"

"Yes, of course, they're real," George said indignantly, and then she turned to Lenny and begged, "Buy me some like that too, Sweetie, please, please, please!"

"I think you've spent enough today, don't you?" he asked mildly, but she pouted and said, "Oh Lenny, don't be so mean!" Gertrude was then rather amused to see that he had caved in and bought her the same pair which she wore triumphantly at dinner the following night. It was the night of George's birthday, and he had spent the day in the casino as usual but had come back early and had a dip in the pool, and now he was in a happy mood and ordered a bottle of champagne to celebrate. He had made love to her that night, and she had snuggled up to him afterwards and said, "I've missed you, George, I wish we could always be like this."

"I do too baby, but business has to come first I'm afraid."

By day four, Gertrude was thoroughly bored and was ready to pack her bags and go home, and she missed Peter. After breakfast, she decided that she would give him a call, but she had forgotten the time difference, and he was already in his bed. "Yes, Mum, I'm having a really good time, and of course, I miss you," he had replied sleepily to her questions, and then, reassured that all was well, she went downstairs to seek out George.

"Can we do something together today? Just the two of us?" she asked hopefully.

"Like what?" he enquired. "What do you have in mind?"

"Maybe we could go and see the Grand Canyon? They do helicopter flights, and you get to see absolutely everything. I've heard it's breath-taking."

"I hate those contraptions," George muttered, "but you go if you want to."

"I don't want to go on my own," she sighed, and he patted her cheek and said, "Never mind love, we'll go and see a show tonight. You'd like that wouldn't you?" She nodded, and he added, "And it'll be a good excuse to show off those earrings I bought you!"

He was as good as his word, and after dinner, they took a cab to see one of the variety shows that Las Vegas was famous for. Lenny and Caroline had decided that they would join them, and they sat down at a small table with a good view of the stage and ordered their cocktails. The drinks were served by a tall, beautifully made-up waitress, but when Lenny playfully goosed her, she said gruffly, "I wouldn't do that Honey, you might find more than you were expecting." Lenny blushed, and Caroline remarked thoughtlessly, "She's got a very deep voice for a woman, hasn't she?"

"That's because she's a man!" laughed George. "They're all men in drag."

"Well, he, or she, certainly fooled me," said Lenny ruefully, "and I'm never going to live this down, am I?"

The show was slick and entertaining, with a magician performing tricks and moving from one table to another, a comedian who did impressions that made them all roar with laughter, and of course the obligatory song and dance act.

Then, just before the finale, a heavily made-up woman with purple hair and a giant poodle dyed to match appeared on the stage. She introduced herself as Madame Zaza and told them that her dog was psychic, and she would channel the messages that came through him. They walked slowly among the tables, and when the dog sat down she would relay a message to a person on that table.

Suddenly the dog sat down by their table and the woman said, "I have a message here for Rudi." No one moved, and so then she tried again. "I have a man here called Roy and he has a message here for Rudi, or maybe it could be Trudy."

"That's me!" cried Gertrude. "He was my first husband." The woman put her hand on the dog's head and then said, "Roy says to take good care of Peter. So, who is Peter, Honey?"

"He's my son," Gertrude replied nervously.

"And does he have a motorcycle?" the woman asked her.

"No, he rides a bicycle. He's far too young for a motorbike."

"Well, Roy says to make sure he always wears his crash hat. It's very important." Gertrude thanked her and patted the dog, who then moved to another table, but the message had disturbed her. She knew that Peter didn't have his bike with him. It had been her present to him on his fourteenth birthday, and she trusted that he wouldn't be messing about on someone else's bicycle. Usually, she would dismiss those claims from clairvoyants as clever trickery, but the woman had been so specific with the names.

"It's all utter rubbish you know," said George airily, but Caroline said, "Oh no, I believed her, she gave me goosebumps, and how on earth did she know all those names?" George shrugged, and then he quickly changed the subject, as he always did when he didn't know the answer to a question.

Soon their holiday was over, and Gertrude was very happy to be going home. While she was getting ready in the bathroom, George slipped a small package into her suitcase, making sure it was well hidden among her clothes. When they landed at Heathrow, he said to her, "Better give me those diamond earrings, Gertie. I'll declare them in customs, and you go through the other channel and wait for me by the barrier."

"Why can't I come with you George?" she asked in surprise, but he snapped, "Because I said so! Now just do as you're told and wait outside."

When he came out, he looked relieved and hugged her, saying, "Sorry Gertie, I just put a few extra fags in your case, and I didn't want the customs men to find them." It wasn't till they were sitting in the tube that she realised it didn't make any sense. Why would he smuggle cigarettes when the duty on them would have been less on than the diamond earrings? She decided it was probably wiser to keep her thoughts to herself.

When they got home, George took the cases upstairs, but when he came down he was as white as a sheet. "Did you take a package out of one of the suitcases?" He asked her, but Gertrude shook her head and told him she hadn't touched the cases since they had left Las Vegas. He sat down and poured himself a stiff whisky and his hand was shaking as he said, "There was $40,000 in your case, and now it's gone." Gertrude was shocked and asked, "How come you had all that money?"

"I won it, of course," George said abruptly. "The thing is, I owe a bloke twelve grand, and if I don't pay it soon I'll be in the shit, big time. I'm so sorry Gertie, but I'm going to have to pawn all your jewellery and I need to borrow all the money that you've got in your account."

"Okay then, take it if you must," Gertrude said dubiously, "but when do you think I will get it back?"

"I don't know; it's going to take quite a while to sort things out. How much have you got?"

"About £2000 give or take a hundred," she told him, but George looked at her with horror and said, "Is that all? That's nowhere near enough. What about Peter's account?"

"He's got almost £5000, but I can't touch that," Gertrude told him.

"Why the hell not?" George frowned. "It'll get me out of trouble. I promise you, he'll get it all back before too long."

"It's not that George. The money's in a trust fund until he's eighteen and no one can touch it till then." He was quiet for a minute and walked over to the window and rested his head against the glass and then asked, "What happens to the money if he doesn't reach eighteen?" Gertrude was shaken and said, "How can you even think that George?"

"Sorry, I was only wondering." He ran a hand through his hair and said, "I didn't mean to upset you, Gertie, it was just a thought."

"Well, I suppose if something did happen to Peter, that money would come to me," Gertrude told him sharply, "but you can forget about it because he's fit and healthy, and I'll make sure he stays that way." She went upstairs and opened her jewellery box and dumped all the stuff on the bed. Then she picked out her wedding and engagement rings from her first husband, Roy. There was no way she was going to let George have those, nor her gold heart-shaped locket that her mother had given her on her eighteenth birthday. Quickly, she wrapped them in a handkerchief and hid them in one of the toes of her boots, then putting everything else back in the box, she took it downstairs and gave it to George.

"Thanks, Gertie, it means a lot, and I'll try and get it all back for you very soon," he said, and then looked pointedly at her engagement ring. "I'm sorry Babe, but I'm going to need that as well." She slipped it off her finger and gave it to him and he had the grace to look rather shame-faced, but when she was about to remove her wedding ring he said, "No, you keep hold of that Gertie, I won't take that from you."

George then disappeared into his study, and she could hear him talking on the phone for ages. Eventually, he reappeared and said abruptly, "I've got to go out, don't wait up."

"Where are you going?" Gertrude cried. "I've got the dinner ready," but he said tersely, "I'm not hungry," and slammed the door behind him.

Chapter 12

George began to roughly assess the total value of Gertrude's jewellery. The diamond engagement ring had originally cost him over £2000, but he knew that he would only get back half of its value. The rest of the stuff would probably fetch another thousand. As he sorted through the collection of gold, he realised that the diamond dollar sign earrings were missing. He had paid a lot for them in Las Vegas, and they would be worth at least another £1000, and he hoped to God that she hadn't lost them.

He was cursing himself for having been so stupid as to put all the money in one case. They had had to wait quite a long time for their cases to emerge on the conveyer belt at Heathrow, and he had fretted impatiently for them to appear. It must have happened then, as he had watched the cases like a hawk at the hotel and had personally loaded them into the taxicab, and the airport wasn't nicknamed 'Thiefrow' for nothing. He would know better next time if there was a next time. He totalled up the money and altogether, with the money from Gertrude's account, it added up to £5000. If he could borrow another couple of grand from Lenny, it would buy him some time to scrape together the rest of the money.

He approached Lenny straight away and said, "Look mate, I'm in a bit of a fix. The money that I won in Las Vegas and that was supposed to pay the dealer, was nicked en route, and I need to borrow a couple of grand. I'll pay you back as soon as I can." Lenny, however, had just had to pay a massive bill on his credit card that he'd foolishly allowed Caroline to use, and was very short of cash himself.

"Sorry George, I'd like to be able to help you out," Lenny said ruefully, "but I haven't got it, mate. I could sell a few shares and let you have the money in a couple of weeks, but I'm a bit short of the readies at the moment."

"What about Caroline's jewellery? There must be a few grands' worth there?"

"It's all in the bank, I'm afraid. She always puts it in her safety deposit box whenever we go away, and she's got the only key."

"Could you ask her if she'd let me have some of it?" George asked hopefully. "I'd pay her back as soon as, and you know I'm good for it." But Lenny just gave him an old-fashioned look and said, "I can try George, but I think she'd rather cut off her arm than part with her bling." George frowned and turned away, saying, "Sorry to have bothered you, Lenny." As he watched his friend drive away, he realised that he'd never seen George look scared before.

George tried to get the money from a few of his other associates, and most wanted to help him but were short of cash themselves. He managed to raise another £1600, and he hoped that together with what he already had, would buy him some time with the drug dealers.

He met up with them the following day and gave them what he had and then promised to get the rest as soon as he could. "Not good enough, George," the dealer told him. "You've got until the end of the week. Don't let me down!" George knew he could not get hold of the money by then, and he realised that his life was, potentially, now in danger. It wasn't the amount, that was simply chicken feed to them, but it was the principle of reneging on a debt. They could make an example of him, or else they could harm Gertrude in some way.

Suddenly, a plan began to form in his mind. If he was able to get rid of Peter and somehow blame it on the drug dealer, he would then benefit from his trust fund. Although he would not be able to get the money straight away, it would buy him precious time if the police arrested the dealer. The other alternative, if the first plan did not work, was to resort to armed robbery. He decided to phone an old associate of his, a petty criminal who was up for anything providing the money was tempting enough. "Tony, it's George here. I've got a little job for you. Meet me in the Red Lion in half an hour."

Tony Taylor was a little weasel of a man with an eyelid that drooped so that quite often people mistakenly thought he was winking at them. He was a career criminal who would do anything for money, and that included murder, and he'd spent plenty of time inside, so prison held no worries for him. It was no worse really than some of the places he'd dossed down in, and at least he got three square meals a day inside. He was already at the bar when George arrived, and he looked with distaste at the sprinkling of dandruff that dusted Tony's shoulders, but if he needed something done, then his man could be relied on, providing that the price was right. Once George had bought their drinks, he took him into a quiet corner to explain what he wanted him to do. "Okay boss, what's going on?" Tony asked eagerly, knowing that if George wanted to see him then there was money involved.

"I want you to get rid of my stepson," George said quietly. "Get hold of a vehicle and knock him off his bike, but I don't want you to make it look like an accident as I want that scumbag drug dealer to get the blame." Tony sucked his teeth and said, "It'll cost you."

"How much?" George asked.

"Three grand," Tony said, his eyes glittering expectantly.

"The maximum I can go to is two thousand," George told him, and Tony countered, "Okay, pay me the two grand now, and then give me another £500 in a month."

"It's a deal," George said, "but it needs to be done tomorrow or the next day at the latest." They shook hands on the deal and Tony asked, "How will I recognise him?"

"He's got a Las Vegas pennant on the back of his bike, and he'll be wearing a yellow cycle helmet, and he gets out of school at three forty-five, so don't be late!"

Next, George went to his bank and opened his safety deposit box and there was only one thing in it. Carefully, he lifted out the gun and unwrapped the cloth and checked to see if it was loaded. It weighed heavily in his hands, and he stroked the barrel, admiring its shape, before wrapping it up again and stowing it in his briefcase. Back at home, he hid it behind some books in his study, knowing it would be quite secure and that Gertrude would not come across it if by any chance he had forgotten to lock up.

Chapter 13

Gertrude was relieved and happy to see Peter back home and safe and sound. He had thoroughly enjoyed his stay with Alice and seemed to have grown by a couple of inches in that short space of time. He'd also managed to catch up with many of his old friends. One evening, Alice had let him style her hair, and she had asked him if he had a girlfriend, but he had shrugged and said, "Not really. I've got girls who are my friends, but they're not girlfriends in the way you mean."

"What about boyfriends?" she had asked, but he had blushed and didn't answer, and she had laughed and said, "It's nothing to be ashamed of if you prefer boys to girls."

"Well…" he hesitated a moment, then said, "there is a boy I like, but I don't think he feels the same way."

"You'll meet someone one day, don't worry," Alice assured him, "but in the meantime, just go out and have fun and enjoy yourself."

"How come you never got married, Aunt Alice?" Peter asked her, and she shrugged and replied, "I guess I never met a man I wanted to marry." There had been someone she had fallen in love with once, but he was already married. She couldn't tell Peter that it was his father, Roy. Gertrude had always known that Alice fancied Roy, and she used to tease her about it from time to time, but apart from a drunken kiss at a party, there was nothing between them. Roy adored Gertrude, and he would never have cheated on her, and Alice knew that.

She decided that if she couldn't have the man she wanted, then she would play the field and enjoy herself, and Alice soon got the reputation as a good-time girl. She was invited to every party, and never said no, and Gertrude had been concerned and told her to take care that men did not take advantage of her. Alice had laughed and said, "I'm enjoying myself, Trudy. Why shouldn't I have sex with men I fancy? I have all the fun and none of the boring stuff, like having to wash their dirty socks. If I meet Mr Right, well then, I'll be happy to change my ways."

Alice never did meet anyone she wanted to settle down with, but she had wanted a child, and she would have swapped places with Gertrude at the drop of a hat. She loved Peter like a son, and he looked so like Roy, and now they had become very close, and she was glad that he was able to talk to her about anything without embarrassment.

Gertrude told Alice about the conversation she'd had with Caroline in Las Vegas and asked her if she'd ever heard about a fashion model called Gemma. "She was a bit of a junkie and I wondered if George knew anything about it. He told me she had died, but he wouldn't talk about her at all, just clammed up."

"I'll try and find out about her and let you know," Alice promised, and the next day Gertrude had a call from her friend with some disturbing news. "I've found out some information about that model, Gemma, you asked about. She was quite a highly thought of model, but then she became paranoid and said that her husband was trying to get rid of her. She died of a drug overdose, and the verdict was death by misadventure, but some of the papers suggested it was suicide. George was questioned by the police, but they didn't have enough evidence to arrest him for supplying the drugs. Just be careful Trudy, don't get mixed up with anything dodgy."

Gertrude had never seen any evidence of drugs in the house, but that didn't mean that George wasn't mixed up with illegal substances, especially as he always kept his study locked. It was not something she could ask him about, as he kept his business activities very close to his chest, but she would certainly be more aware, and she wondered if perhaps the missing money had possibly been a debt to pay off a drug dealer.

She had brought Peter back a T-shirt from Las Vegas and a pennant to hang on his bedroom wall, and he'd been pleased and said, "That's so cool, Mum, I'll go out and attach it to my bike." She couldn't help but remember the warning she had received from Roy, and so she instilled in Peter the need to always wear his cycle helmet, but if the clairvoyant in Las Vegas had told her what was about to happen, she would have taken Peter and run a mile.

The following Monday, he was back at school. He realised that he would have to knuckle down to do some serious studying for his GCSEs, but was not looking forward to it. Gertrude had not wanted him to take his bike to school, but he had begged and pleaded. Eventually, she had caved in, but only on the condition that he religiously wore his cycle helmet. George was not around much at the moment, going out early in the morning and coming home late at night, but that was just fine as far as Peter was concerned.

On Wednesday, Peter had not come home from school at the usual time and Gertrude was getting anxious. When he still had not arrived by six o'clock she was panicking, but she didn't know who to call, so she phoned George. "Calm down," he told her. "Keep your shirt on Gertie. He's probably just around at a friend's house."

"But he hasn't got any friends around here," she tried to tell him, but with typical impatience, he had already rung off. As she was debating what to do next, the doorbell rang, and she saw a policeman on the porch standing on the step. "Mrs Bellman?" he enquired, and when she affirmed that she was, he said, "Now don't be alarmed, but your son, Peter, has had an accident and has been taken to hospital."

"Oh my God, I knew it! Is he badly hurt?" She cried, her stomach churning, and the constable reassured her that though serious, his injuries were not life-threatening. She called a taxi and drove straight there and prayed all the way that he would be alright. When she saw him on the ward, he looked pale but gave her a wan smile. She was upset to see that he had a broken arm and ankle, and a fractured cheek bone. "Someone knocked me off my bike, Mum," he told her, "and the bastard didn't even stop." Gertrude had a flash of apprehension and wondered if somehow George had something to do with it. She shook off the thought and chided herself for her suspicions, but she thanked her lucky stars that Peter had worn his cycle helmet.

The hospital would keep him in overnight, so she went home and phoned George to let him know what had happened. She would also have to ask him to help her move Peter's bed downstairs as he would not be very mobile for a while. He did not say a great deal about Peter's accident, but he hugged her.

Then he helped her to move the bed down into the conservatory, but after that, he disappeared into his study where he stayed for the rest of the evening making endless phone calls.

The next day, the police told her that a witness had come forward who had seen the accident, except that it didn't appear to be an accident at all. A white van had been seen parked in the street close to the school and when Peter rode past on his bike, the man had started the engine and deliberately swerved and driven into him and then sped off. She would not tell him that, however, as he was under the impression that it had merely been just an unfortunate accident. He would be upset and terrified to think that he had been deliberately targeted.

The woman who had seen it happen had the forethought to take down the number of the van, but it had been reported stolen earlier that day. Unfortunately, she hadn't got a good look at the driver. The police also told her that because Peter was wearing his cycle helmet, it had undoubtedly saved him from more serious injury, or even death. She was eternally grateful that Roy had given that message from beyond the grave.

Chapter 14

Jessica woke each morning in their double bed and sighed with contentment. Usually, Josh, or sometimes Sam, would bring her a cup of tea in the morning and when she had drunk it, she would go and luxuriate in a hot bath until the water started to cool. It was such bliss to be in a place that was warm and comfortable, and where one didn't have to regulate life to the infrequent periods of when the electricity was working.

After breakfast, Josh helped her to clear the plates and she looked fondly at her son. He was growing so fast, and she ruffled his hair and told him, "I need to cut your hair, you're beginning to look like a Shetland pony."

"Neigh!" Josh whinnied and then galloped around the kitchen before disappearing outside and leaping around the garden. Jess smiled, he was still such a child, but not for much longer. She sighed as she wondered what sort of future lay ahead of him.

They had all gone to the pub on Boxing Day leaving Buster in charge, patrolling the garden, and Jess had got re-acquainted with some of the neighbours. Most of the people were friendly in the village, and it was such a relief to be able to stroll down the street and not have to be constantly on the alert for danger. It was a bright and sunny day, if rather cold, and the sunlight made the ice crystals on the trees sparkle like diamonds, and here and there a squirrel or a robin rustled among the dry leaves, searching for food in the undergrowth. All her tension had now dissipated, and she felt relaxed and at her ease, but she was very glad of the warm scarf that Sam had given her for Christmas.

When they arrived at the pub, they noticed two poorly dressed young men hanging around outside who were drinking the dregs out of the glasses that other people had left behind. Sam immediately recognised them as the two young lads who had tried to steal his eggs. He felt very sorry for them, as they had no money to spend on themselves, so he asked them if they would like a drink. They looked up in surprise, and said: "Yes please, Mister, that's very good of you."

Sam went to the bar and ordered two pints of beer and some turkey sandwiches and took them out to the boys. They couldn't believe that he would treat them after they had tried to steal from him, and felt rather embarrassed by his kindness, but Sam said, "Look, I know that times are hard, but in the Spring if you're interested, I can let you have half a dozen bantams."

"Really?" They both looked at him incredulously.

"Yeah, it'll give you a start and you can make a bit of money selling the eggs around the village, and I'll help you build a coop if you like. I've got some spare netting at home."

They were amazed and grateful and promised him that they would not get into trouble again, but Jessica was incredulous that Sam would treat a pair of thieving boys so generously. "They're not bad lads, Jess," Sam told her. "They're just poor and hungry, and everyone deserves a second chance, and I'd like to help them keep on the right path."

"Oh Sam, you're so good, and you care about people," she told him and thought how lucky she was to have found such a kind and considerate husband.

Jessica had spent most of the holidays catching up on her reading and playing games with Josh. He was really getting the hang of chess, even beating Sam on a couple of occasions. Now, however, it was nearly time to go back to London, and she felt utterly despondent. "Try not to think about it," Sam had told her, but it was no good, she simply could not stop her mind from worrying. She was simply dreading going back and having to face the daily power cuts and the dark, and dangerous walk from her place of work to her home.

She wondered how Gertrude was getting on, and whether she'd had some company over the Christmas holidays. She hoped that she hadn't been on her own, and she would remember to take her back some fresh eggs and a jar of honey, and she would also take one for Gregor, as he had been so kind to Josh.

New Year's Eve, they again spent at their local pub along with most of the inhabitants of the village. The pub had laid on a special hog roast, along with mulled wine and spiced beer. There was a good show of fireworks at the end of the night, and everyone was in a happy, jolly mood except for Jess. No trains were running on New Year's Day, but she had to be back at work on the second of January, and so Sam had paid one of the local farmers who was taking his produce to market in Swindon to give Jess a lift and drop her off at the station.

She would have to rise at four o'clock to be able to catch the 8.30 train and she would hopefully be at her desk before lunchtime. The company would fine her half a day's pay of course, but it was worth it to her to have the extra two days to spend with Sam and Josh. Sam walked with her to the pub where the lorry would pick her up, and Jess could not stop crying. "I'm sorry Sam," she apologised, but he held her close and said, "I wish there was some way I could pay for you to get out of your contract, but I'm afraid it would take a miracle."

The lorry arrived, and Sam helped her clamber up into the cab. He'd left Josh still asleep, and Jess had said a tearful goodbye to him the night before. "Don't worry, Mum," he had told her, "it'll soon be the Easter holidays and we'll see each other then." He had no concept of what she went through each day, and she prayed that when he grew up he would never have to live through such tough times.

The lorry driver was taciturn, and Jess was not in the mood to chat either, so they hurtled through the country lanes in silence. It had snowed a little in the night, but now it began to fall in earnest, and the driver had to slow his speed, but they managed to arrive at Swindon station with ten minutes to spare before the 8.30 train was due. However, as Jess walked onto the platform, there was an announcement that owing to heavy snowdrifts further up the line there would be no trains at all that day.

Jess realised that she would have to find somewhere to spend the night, but the hotel near the station had no vacancies, so she began to trudge through the snowy streets in the hope of finding a B&B. After she had spent an hour searching, she realised that she was ravenously hungry as she'd had no breakfast, and so she turned into the first café she came across and ordered a steaming mug of tea and a full English fry up.

Feeling warmed and refreshed, she continued her hunt for somewhere to spend the night, but after another couple of hours of fruitless searching, she realised it was hopeless. Many travellers had also tried to find accommodation for the duration, and everywhere was full. In despair, she went back to the station and found that a few people were hanging around on the platform, but luckily the waiting room was open. She managed to squeeze herself into a small space on one of the benches and resigned herself to spending the night there.

There was a stove burning in the waiting room, but it was not throwing out a great deal of heat. After a while, Jessica's feet were numb with the cold. She had bought some biscuits for the journey, but after a couple of hours, she felt peckish so took out the packet and opened it. It would have been churlish not to offer any to her neighbouring travellers, so they were soon gone. Eventually, she needed to go to the bathroom, and so asked the woman next to her to keep her seat and to look after her trolley. The lavatory was none too clean, but needs must, and Jess made sure to wash her hands thoroughly afterwards. She caught her reflection in the mirror and almost burst out laughing, as she resembled some poor old bag lady whom she would have tossed a coin to if she had found her in a doorway. On her return, her neighbour decided that she too needed to brave the facilities, and Jess reciprocated and kept her place for her on the bench.

It was growing dark, but the strip light in the waiting room was not giving a lot of light and Jess found it was a strain to try and read her book. The woman next to her asked her where she worked, but Jess did not want to say that she worked for a loan and debt collecting company, so she just said that she worked in an office in Chiswick. She told her that she was contracted to work for another three years and that she was having to live apart from her husband and son for most of the year. "That must be very hard on you," her neighbour said, and Jess nodded. "Yes, it is. I pray to win the lottery every week, but so far I haven't won anything at all."

"Well, maybe luck will be on your side this week," the woman laughed, and Jess asked her, "What about you? Do you work?"

"Yes, I work in a department store on Oxford Street, but I'm not sure whether I'll still have a job when I get back. They're laying off a lot of people. All the foreign visitors the shops used to rely on, are no longer able to come, and far fewer people can afford to buy new goods these days."

"What will you do?" asked Jess, and the woman shrugged. "Well, I'll try to find another job of course, but it's getting more and more difficult to find any kind of work. My husband still has a job contract, but we'll have to tighten our belts and I may be forced to take in a lodger."

"Well, there are plenty of homeless people," Jess said, but the woman snorted. "Oh no, I would only take in a professional person. If you take in one of the homeless, you would have to take whoever the council sent you, and I want to have a say in who I invite into my home."

"I don't blame you," said Jess, as some of the homeless people she'd seen hanging around on the street had looked very scary. She thought that very soon the councils would begin to make people take in lodgers if they had a spare room, as the situation was becoming more and more desperate.

After a while, Jess felt very weary and rested her arms on the handle of her trolley and her head on her arms. She managed to sleep fitfully for a couple of hours, but then she woke with an aching back and a crick in her neck. The stove had gone out and it was bitterly cold, and she would have given anything for a steaming hot mug of tea. She looked at her watch and groaned as it was only four o'clock and the first train was not due until six-thirty if it was even running. The woman beside her was asleep with her mouth open, snoring gently, but the man on her other side was awake and attempting to do the crossword. "Are you any good at cryptic clues?" he asked her, and Jess said, "Sometimes, but it does rather depend on the setter."

"What about this one, Sunday concert involved jigs and reels, seven and six letters?"

"It's something dances, I think," said Jess, and then realised that it was an anagram. "It's country dances!"

"Great, that fits. You are good at this." He complimented her. Trying to attempt to solve the clues helped to take Jessica's mind off her discomfort, and before they knew it, they heard the announcement of the arrival of the first train. She managed to find a seat and then spent the best part of the journey worrying about what her boss would say. She arrived at work thirty minutes late, but before she'd even taken off her coat she was summoned with a roar, "Mrs Jones, my office, now!" The manager didn't even bother to look up as she entered, just said, "You're twenty-four hours and thirty minutes late."

"Yes, I know, but there were no trains because of the snow," Jess said in a tremulous voice, fighting back the tears. The manager looked up then, and folding his hands over his massive paunch, leant back in his chair said, "That's not my problem. You can leave now and collect your cards and any wages owing to you on the way out."

"You're sacking me?" Jess asked, stunned that he could be so uncaring. "But I spent the whole night in a station waiting room, and you know I would have got here if I could."

"As I said, not my problem," he sneered, "so you'd better go home and get your head down, hadn't you?"

"I don't think you can sack me for this," protested Jess angrily, longing to tip him backwards in his chair and wipe that smug look from his face, but he replied, "Oh I think you'll find I can! After all, it's not the first time you've been late back for work, is it Mrs Jones? Now, are you going without a fuss, or do I have to call security?"

"I'm going," Jess said, biting back the words that she wanted to spit at him, as she would most probably be needing a reference from him at some stage. She gathered together her things quickly and headed for the door, holding her head high, trying not to cry in front of her colleagues, whose pitying looks just made her feel worse.

Chapter 15

As Gertrude continued to leaf through her photo album, she remembered how she had discovered that it was George who was behind her son's accident. It was a couple of days after Peter had come home from the hospital and George had gone out to the car to fetch some paperwork. He had carelessly left his mobile phone on the kitchen table. When it pinged to show that he had a text, Gertrude could not help herself but read it. Then, as the realisation hit her that it was George who was responsible for Peter's accident, she felt sick to her stomach. The text said, "I wnt my dosh. Nt my falt boy's alive, did job ok, wnt pay NOW. T."

Gertrude's hand flew to her mouth, and she ran to the sink and retched, but on hearing George return she quickly ran the taps and, taking out a scouring pad, began to vigorously clean the draining board. With a supreme effort, she kept her voice level and said, "I think you had a text just now." He picked up the phone and read the message, his face grim, then put the phone in his pocket. "Who's it from?" Gertrude asked casually, but he replied, "No one important, it's just business. I've got to go out now, so don't bother with dinner for me, I'll be eating in town." As he left, he gave her a peck on the cheek, and it took all her willpower not to recoil from his touch.

She watched him drive away and then she picked up the phone and called the police to tell them about the message she had read on her husband's phone. They told her that they would send someone as soon as possible to the house to speak to her. She waited nervously until she saw a police car stop outside and, checking that Peter was in the lounge listening to music on his headphones, she showed the officers into the kitchen.

"So, Mrs Bellman," the detective asked her, "apart from the text, do you have any other evidence that your husband was behind the attempt on your son's life?"

"No, not exactly evidence," Gertrude confided, "but I do know that he owes someone a lot of money. He wanted to borrow Peter's savings, but it's in a trust fund until he's eighteen. George asked me what would happen to the money if Peter died, and I thought that was rather an odd thing to ask."

"Yes, it does seem rather strange," the policeman agreed. "Peter is your son from your first marriage I take it?"

"Yes, my first husband died and left me the house in Kew and a lump sum of money. George wanted me to sell the house and put the money into a joint account, but I refused, and he was quite annoyed. I've rented out the house, and half the money goes into Peter's trust fund and the other half to me. George took all my money and jewellery, but he said it was nowhere near enough for what he needed to pay his debts."

"How does George get on with your son?"

"They don't get on at all," Gertrude said sadly. "Peter hates him, and George thinks that I spoil him, but I'm only looking out for him like any mother would."

"What does your husband do Mrs Bellman?"

"Do you mean what work does he do?" Gertrude asked, having never bothered to ask him. Somehow, she instinctively felt that it was better not to know.

"Yes, how does he make a living?"

"I've no idea really." Gertrude shrugged. "He says he wheels and deals, whatever that means. He's forever locking himself in his study, especially when he has some of his cronies coming around. He doesn't like me to disturb him."

"Would you recognise any of them again?" the detective asked her.

"Yes, I think so. I only really know Lenny Thomas and his wife, Caroline, as they came to Las Vegas with us. George won a lot of money, but he put it in the suitcase and when we got home it had gone. He was livid, and that's why he's having to scrabble around for money now."

"Is the study locked now?"

"Yes, I think so, he usually locks it, but you can try the door." It was locked, and there was no spare key. The detective asked Gertrude if she would go to the police station and look at some photos to see if she could recognise any of George's associates. She told Peter that she was going out for an hour or so. The police gave her a lift to the station where she scrolled through their computer's mug shots. After a while, she thought she recognised one of the men and said, "This chap's been to the house once or twice to see George. I'm pretty sure it's him as he has a droopy eye."

"That's Tony Taylor," the detective told her. "He's a petty criminal who's been in prison, so we'll talk to him, Mrs Bellman, and see what we come up with. We'll keep you informed."

"You won't tell George I've spoken to you, will you?" Gertrude asked anxiously.

"No, of course not, but if I were you, I'd get your son out of harm's way. Maybe he could stay with a friend?" The policeman suggested.

"Yes, that's a good idea," Gertrude agreed. "I know my friend Alice would look after him."

She spoke to Alice as soon as she got home, and her friend said she'd be glad to have him stay. Gertrude told her that she would explain everything once they got there. To Peter, she just said, "I'm taking you to stay with Alice for a few days as there's going to be a lot of upheaval and comings and goings in the house. I want you to be safely out of the way for the time being."

"There's no need, I'll be alright here, Mum," he told her when she made her suggestion that he should go away for a while, but she asked, "I thought that you liked being with Alice?"

"Yes, of course, I do, you know I do."

"Well then, go pack your stuff and we'll go this afternoon, and no arguments." He knew better than to protest when his mother had that tone of voice. He got his things together without further ado. Gertrude took a cab as Peter was still none too steady on his crutches. Once he was settled in front of the TV at Alice's flat, she took her friend into the kitchen and confided that she suspected George was behind the accident. She told her about the text she had seen on his phone and that the police were checking things out, and Alice was horrified and begged her, "Don't go back to him Trudy, stay here with me."

"I have to go back, otherwise George will be suspicious, but don't tell Peter any of this, will you?" Alice agreed to keep quiet but warned her friend to be very careful and to keep her informed of anything else that transpired.

Gertrude was just on her way up to bed when George arrived home. He'd been drinking, she could smell it on his breath from a metre away, and she knew that when he'd had a drink, he became amorous.

"Come here Gertie, give us a kiss," he had grinned and had grabbed her bottom.

"I'm tired George," she had protested, pushing him away, but he was having none of it. "I know just how to wake you up, come here!" The trouble was he did know exactly how to get her aroused, and her body reacted despite her feelings of loathing for him. He was a good lover, and soon she was lost in a passionate embrace, hating him but wanting his body, until at last, they finished with an explosive climax. He immediately rolled over and went to sleep, snoring gently, but she stayed awake for a long time, despising herself for giving in to her needs, but also worrying about what the police would come up with.

George had already left the house the following morning when Gertrude woke. He turned up unexpectedly around midday looking rather pale and tense. "Gertie, hurry up and go upstairs and pack a few things. We need to go away for a few days," he commanded but she looked puzzled and asked him, "Why, what's going on George?"

"I'll explain later. Just get a move on will you." She ran upstairs and began to throw a few things into a suitcase, but then suddenly the police arrived mob-handed and began banging on the door. If she had not opened it smartly, they would have broken it down.

"George Bellman, I'm arresting you for the attempted murder of Peter Adams," the police officer told him. "You don't have to say anything, but what you do say may be used in evidence against you." As he put the handcuffs on him, George stared hard at Gertrude and hissed, "It was you who stitched me up, wasn't it?"

"Yes," Gertrude retorted, "I saw the text on your phone and told the police. You should be thoroughly ashamed to have targeted an innocent boy. I hope they lock you up for good!"

He glared at her, his dark eyes full of hate, and he would never forgive her for her betrayal of him, and his parting words were, "I'll get even with you if it's the last thing I do!"

The police had brought a sniffer dog with them, and they searched the house from top to bottom. The dog had found traces of drugs in George's study and then they removed his laptop and mobile phones. By a lucky stroke, one of the officers came across the gun that had been hidden behind some books. When they had gone, Gertrude felt an overwhelming sense of relief, but she had some unexpected and unwelcome visitors that night and once again, she was plunged into a terrifying scenario.

She had just gone to bed when there was a loud, persistent hammering at the front door, and she crept downstairs, her heart beating ten to the dozen, and called, "Who is it?"

"Open up," a gruff male voice commanded, "or else we'll break the bloody door down!" Terrified, she opened the door to see two burly men on the step who rudely pushed past her and demanded, "Where's that bastard, George?"

"He's been arrested," Gertrude stammered. "The police took him away this morning."

"He owes us a lot of money, and if we don't get it then we'll have to just take what we want."

"Take it all, I don't care," Gertrude said, "I don't want anything more to do with him." The men rampaged through the house taking anything of value and then demanded his car keys.

"I think he's got those with him, but there might be a spare set in his study," she told them, and after a thorough search, they located a set in a cough sweet tin in his desk drawer.

When they had gone, she was far too wound up to sleep, so she began to pack all her and Peter's belongings. Then in the morning, she called a cab to take her to Alice's flat, and the first thing she did was to file for divorce.

Chapter 16

Gertrude had not gone to George's trial. She had been told that there was no need to call her as a witness and she didn't want to see him or have any more to do with him. She had been forced to visit him once after the court appearance to ask him to sign divorce papers, but he had flatly refused and had been very nasty to her, blaming her for his predicament. His parting shot to her had been "I'll come looking for you when I get out, and I'll make you sorry you were ever born!"

George got ten years for attempted murder and five for drug dealing, and he had lost everything. His house had been repossessed and his car and any items of value had been taken by the drug dealers to whom he owed the money. Gertrude then decided that she would now sell her house in Kew and buy a small flat for her and Peter. As for the present time, they were staying with Alice, and it was proving to be rather a squeeze.

Because of Peter's injuries, he had been unable to sit his exams, but Alice had asked him if he wanted to train to be a hairdresser, as he was always trying out different styles on her and her long-suffering friends. He confided to her that it was what he wanted to do with his life. She told him that a friend of hers owned a salon in Chiswick and she would have a word with him to see if he would take him on as an apprentice. Peter naturally jumped at the chance, and Gertrude decided to look for a flat in the Chiswick area so that he would be near his work, and eventually found the flat that would one day become her prison.

Peter had loved living at Alice's, even though with the three of them it was rather cramped, and he was relieved to be rid of George's malign presence. She had arranged for him to have the interview with her friend who owned a hair salon. He had agreed to take Peter on as an apprentice with two afternoons off a week to attend college. He wasn't paid a lot, but he didn't care because he was doing what he loved, and he was a hard-working and willing pupil.

He had been taken under the wing of one of the girls who had decided to give him a make-over, cutting his hair in the latest style and giving him blonde highlights, and he had been thrilled with his new image. One of the young men at the salon soon began to take an interest in him, recognising him as a fellow gay man, and he asked him if he'd like to go to a gay bar with him at the weekend. Peter had never been anywhere like that before, and he had asked Alice what he should do. "Do you like the guy?" she asked him, and he shrugged and said, "I like him well enough, but not in that way."

"Then tell him you like him just as a mate but go to the bar for a drink with him anyway. You might meet someone there that you like."

When Peter and his friend arrived at the bar, it was heaving, with loud music making it hard to be understood. They pushed their way over to the bar, and as the barman took their order, Peter could not take his eyes off him. He was young, blonde, and Australian, with a handsome, cheerful-looking face. He smiled at Peter and said, "Hi, I'm Wayne. I've not seen you in here before, have I?"

"No, this is my first time."

"You are over eighteen, aren't you?" he asked, and Peter assured him that he was, but Wayne asked if he had any ID. Peter shook his head, but his friend said, "I can vouch for him. We work together, and I know he's telling the truth."

"No worries." Wayne grinned. "You two just have a good time."

They sat at the bar, looking around and sipping their drinks. Then his friend asked Peter if he wanted to dance, but he was suddenly overcome with shyness and declined. His friend asked, "You don't mind if I do, this rhythm gets to me, and I can't sit still. I love dancing."

"No, you go ahead," Peter reassured him, "I'm quite happy watching." He looked on as his friend gyrated on the dance floor, a little envious that he could move so unselfconsciously, but then he turned back to the bar and drank his beer quickly. He couldn't take his eyes off the Australian barman, who came over to refill his glass and said, "Take it easy mate, that stuff's a lot stronger than it looks."

He noticed a couple of guys kissing in the corner and wondered what it would be like to kiss Wayne. He had nicely shaped lips, full, but not too full, and perfect teeth and just the thought gave Peter a little thrill. After a while, a couple of guys asked him to dance, but he said no to both of them. After starting on his third pint of strong lager, Peter needed to use the toilet, and he pushed his way through the throng of dancers to the gents. His head felt a little woozy, and he decided that after he had finished his pint, he would head for home.

Peter returned to the bar, but after a few more sips of his drink the room started spinning, and then he passed out. Then, one of the men who had asked him to dance earlier hurried over and attempted to help him to his feet, but Wayne intervened and said, "It's okay, I'll get his mate to give him a hand," but the man was quite insistent that he would take care of him.

Wayne hurriedly pushed his way over to Peter's companion and said, "You'd better hurry, I think your little friend's drink's been spiked." As they made their way through the crowd they saw that the man was half carrying and half dragging Peter's limp form towards the exit.

"Oi, what are you doing to my mate?" His friend shouted, but the man turned and said glibly, "I was just taking him out for some air."

"Well, I've got him now, so you can do one, okay?" The guy shrugged and let go of Peter, and then Wayne suggested that he call a taxi so that his friend could take him home, but he replied, "I would, but I don't know where he lives. We only work together."

"I've got a room upstairs, and I suppose we could take him up there and let him sleep it off." They struggled up the stairs with him and laid him on the bed, and then Wayne had to hurry back down to the bar.

The next morning, Peter woke and had no idea where he was. He sat up groggily and then saw the Australian barman doing press-ups wearing just his underpants. He could not help but be impressed by his fit, well-muscled body. He realised that at some time during the night he had been undressed apart from his pants, and then Wayne grinned and said, "Ah, it lives! How are you feeling mate?"

"A bit groggy, and my head's banging."

"A couple of aspirin and a hot shower should do the trick."

"What happened? Did you undress me?" Peter wanted to know, and Wayne nodded, and he asked shyly, "Did you…you know?"

"Of course not!" Wayne said indignantly. "Your drink was spiked, and for the record, I like my lovers to be fully conscious."

"Sorry," Peter said, feeling chastened. "It was very kind of you to take care of me."

"No worries. Now, how about taking that shower?" Peter hesitated, and Wayne grinned, "Come on lazy-bones," and pulled off the duvet. Then his grin widened, and he said, "Ah, I see we have a little stiffy! What are we going to do about that then?"

"I…I need the toilet," Peter stammered and dashed for the bathroom.

When he reappeared Wayne asked, "Are you a virgin Peter?"

"'Course not," he said indignantly, "I've had sex loads of times."

"There's no shame in being a virgin, you know," Wayne told him gently. "Everybody in the world was at some point, even me! Now, how about that shower?"

Wayne followed him into the shower and then began to soap him all over. When he was clean, knelt in front of him, and Peter had never known such ecstasy, and he could not stop smiling. This gorgeous man had wanted him, and he felt as though he were ten feet tall. "You have such a great body, Wayne. Do you go to the gym?" he asked, and the barman nodded. "Yeah, twice a week. You can come with me next time if you like."

Peter was madly in love with Wayne but confided to Alice that he couldn't see what someone as gorgeous as he was would see in the likes of him, but she assured him, "Sweetie, you're a good-looking young man, and even more so now that you've put on some muscle." He had been going to the gym with Wayne and had noticed that his body shape had improved, but he still felt like an ugly duckling beside his glamourous lover.

The next day, he was in the bathroom morosely squeezing at a spot on his chin when Wayne came in and said, "Don't do that, you'll only spread it." Peter pulled a face and said, "I don't know what you see in me, I'm nothing to write home about, am I?"

"Don't be so silly," Wayne laughed. "Tell me, who wouldn't love that cute little face and that peachy bum?"

"So, you do love me a bit then?"

"I love you a lot," Wayne told him. "Come here, you dummy." He embraced Peter and reassured him, "You're mine, and I love you just as are, spots and all!"

Peter and Wayne saw each other about four times a week. They both went weight training on Monday and Tuesday after work and then went for something to eat. Saturdays were the busiest days for both young men, and Peter often had to work late at the salon. He would go home for a bath and a change of clothes, have something to eat, and then head for the bar where Wayne worked. He would arrive late on in the evening and sit drinking at the bar until closing time, and then help Wayne to clear up. Both of them would be exhausted and would collapse into bed, too tired to make love, but on Sunday they certainly made up for it.

The bar was closed on Mondays, so Peter begged the boss at the salon if he could have his day off on the same day as Wayne so that they could spend more time together. Gertrude and Alice were both dying to meet Peter's lover, so eventually, they arranged to meet up one Sunday at lunchtime at a pub by the river at Kew. It was a warm, sunny day, and the two women had arrived early to ensure a table outside in the sun. Suddenly, Alice nudged Gertrude and said, "Trudy, they're here, and I can see what Peter means; he's a young god!"

Wayne was wearing shorts and a cut-away T-shirt, and he was deeply tanned with his blonde hair stylishly cut by Peter. He had a smile to light up a room, and he beamed and shook hands with Gertrude and said, "It's so nice to meet you, at last, Mrs Adams."

"And I've been looking forward to meeting you Wayne, but my name's not Adams now. I reverted to my maiden name of Trent, but you can call me Trudy."

"Well, Trudy, you certainly don't look old enough to be Peter's mum, and you," he said turning to Alice, "must be Peter's fairy godmother." Alice laughed, "Is that what he told you?"

"He told me you were a very special lady." Gertrude nodded her approval and said, "She certainly is. I don't know how we'd have managed without her."

The boys went to get some drinks and the two women agreed that Wayne was a cut above the usual young men that they had met. Not only was he good-looking, but he had good manners and boundless charm, and he seemed genuinely fond of Peter.

Gertrude asked Wayne where he was from in Australia, and he replied, "I'm from Perth."

"Do you have any brothers or sisters?"

His face suddenly looked pensive, and he told her, "I did have an older sister, but she and my mum both drowned in a boating accident."

"I'm so sorry, how awful for you." Gertrude put a sympathetic hand on his arm. "When did it happen, was it recently?"

"No, it was nearly six years ago. Dad has re-married since and I've got a four-year-old half-sister. She's called Lily and she's really cute."

"How do you get on with your stepmother?"

"We get on fine, and she's not the problem, but Dad is. He never accepted me being gay, and he doesn't have much to do with me anymore."

"I'm sad to hear that," Gertrude told him. "My ex-husband could never accept Peter, and sadly there are still an awful lot of dinosaurs out there."

Chapter 17

The next few months went by very quickly and Peter passed his exams with flying colours. "I'm a fully qualified hairdresser now," he told Wayne proudly, "and I think we should do something to celebrate."

"Sure," Wayne agreed and asked, "what would you like to do?" Peter thought a moment and then said, "I'd like to take you to see Kew gardens. We always used to go there when my dad was alive, and it has some really happy memories for me."

They took a picnic and a cool bag with some beers and when they entered the palm house, Wayne looked around and remarked, "This reminds me of home."

"You're not home-sick, are you?" Peter asked anxiously, and Wayne laughed, "No, mate. The only thing I miss is the sunshine, but we've certainly got Australian weather today!" They walked for hours, eventually stopping under a shady tree to have their lunch, and then tired from walking, they took the tube home and Wayne said, "Thanks for today, Peter. I didn't realise how much I missed the green spaces. It was great to breathe in some fresh air again!"

It was rather crowded living at Alice's place, and Gertrude began to look around for a two-bedroom flat in the Chiswick area. She had put her house in Kew on the market and had soon found a buyer, and once the sale was complete she and Peter would be able to move. She had managed to find an ideal ground-floor flat in a Victorian house that was walking distance from the shops and Peter's place of work, and at last, everything was settled and then they were able to move into their own home.

Neither Peter nor Gertrude could drive, but Wayne had a licence and offered to help. They hired a van and finally got all her furniture out of storage, but Peter kept finding things that he had forgotten about. He would sit engrossed in some old comic books that Gertrude had to remind him more than once to help with shifting the furniture and boxes so that Wayne would be able to return the rental van on time.

It was the following Monday when an official-looking letter arrived for Wayne, and as he read it his face fell and he cried, "No! No, they can't do this to me!" Peter looked up in alarm and asked, "What on earth's happened?"

"It's from the home office and they're saying they won't renew my visa and I've got to go back home." Peter's eyes filled with tears, and he asked, "Can't you appeal?"

"I already did once before, and they extended it then, but they won't do it a second time."

"How long is it till you have to leave?"

"Six weeks," Wayne said sadly, "and I just know the time will fly by."

Peter was sunk in abject misery, and the six weeks would just go by in a flash, but Wayne thought for a while and then said, "There might be a way that we can stay together. How would you feel about coming to Oz with me?"

"What, you mean just for a holiday?"

"No, I mean come over for good. You could apply to the Australian embassy, and as you're now a fully qualified hairdresser they would look favourably on your application, especially if you already had a job to go to."

Peter's face shone, and he asked with incredulity, "Do you mean it? You'd want me to come with you?"

"Of course, I do," Wayne insisted. "I love you Peter, and I want to share my life with you."

"Then, of course, I'll come! But how do I go about applying for a job there?"

"I'll talk to my stepmother," Wayne assured him. "She owns a hair salon and I'm sure she'd give you a job if I begged her."

Wayne waited until Sunday to call home when he reckoned that his father would be out and was relieved when his stepmother answered. "Hi Helen, it's Wayne. How are you all?"

"Just fine, but I'm afraid that your father's not in at present."

"It's you that I wanted to talk to. Helen, I've got to come back home in a few weeks as they won't renew my visa, but the thing is, I've fallen in love and want him to come with me. His name's Peter and he's a very talented hairdresser, so it would be amazing if you could give him a job to help with his application to settle in Oz. What do you say?"

"I'll have to think about it, Wayne. I don't need any more staff at the moment."

"Please Helen, I wouldn't ask you, but I'm desperate. He's the love of my life."

"I'll see what I can do," his stepmother said, "but I'm not going to make any promises."

"Thanks, I know that you'll try. How's Lily doing?" Wayne asked after his half-sister.

"She's fine, but missing you, so she'll be delighted that you're coming home."

"I'll have to bring her a nice gift then. Have you got any ideas of what she'd like?"

"Something to wear maybe. She's grown a fair bit, so get a couple of sizes bigger and anything as long as it's pink." Wayne laughed, "Okay. Say hi to Dad for me."

Peter made his application to the Australian embassy for permanent residence, and they waited anxiously for a reply. In the meantime, Wayne's stepmother had written and offered Peter a job, and Wayne was delighted and grateful that she had put herself out for him, as it would certainly help with Peter's application.

A few days before Wayne's departure, they got confirmation that Peter's application had been accepted. It had helped that he had a job to go to and that he had a few thousand pounds in the bank from his father's legacy. They were thrilled and went out to celebrate, but they hadn't told Gertrude what Peter had planned, just in case he had been refused. They would have upset her needlessly, but now Peter was dreading to have to break the news.

They decided to tell Gertrude and Alice together and invited them out for lunch to an Italian restaurant, and Gertrude asked, "What's the big occasion? Is it your birthday Wayne?"

"No, it's nothing like that. You know that I've got to go back to Australia?"

139

"Yes, Peter told me and I'm so sorry you have to leave." The young men looked at each other, and then Peter blurted out, "Mum, I've decided to go with him."

"You mean go out there for a holiday?"

"No, I mean for good. I've been accepted to settle in Australia and Wayne's step-mum has given me a job in her salon." Gertrude looked at him aghast. She wanted to scream, but somehow she managed to control herself and asked in a voice that shook, "When are you leaving?"

"I'm not sure. Wayne was going first to try and get a job and to find somewhere for us to live, and then send for me to join him, but I don't think I can bear to be apart from him for any length of time." Wayne looked at him in surprise and said, "Do you mean we'll be able to fly out together?"

"Yes, I don't see any point in waiting, do you? Now that I've got a job to go to I'll just find some cheap digs until you get some work, and then we can get our place together if that's okay with you?"

"You bet it is," Wayne crowed, "and I'm over the moon that you're coming with me, and now I can book us on the flight for next week."

"I see." Gertrude gulped, and Alice squeezed her hand under the table, and Gertrude hoped with all her heart that Wayne would change his mind about Peter going out there with him. He was a lovely young man, but she couldn't bear the thought of losing her only son.

As if he'd been able to read her mind, Peter said, "Don't worry, we'll be able to Skype each other every week, Mum, and you can come and visit once we're settled. It'll be an adventure!" That would be an adventure I could do without, thought Gertrude, but she forced herself to smile, putting on a brave face and not wanting to embarrass him. Later, she went home with Alice and cried her eyes out, sobbing, "I can't bear to lose him, Alice."

"You won't be losing him." Alice tried to comfort her. "If he was moving to Scotland, for example, you'd maybe see him only once or twice a year, so it's just a long journey to Australia. You do want him to be happy, don't you?"

"Yes, of course, I do!" Gertrude cried, "but I just wish it wasn't at the other end of the earth."

Alice, too, was very upset at the thought of Peter moving so far away. She loved him and thought of him as her nephew or even a surrogate son. More than anything, she wanted him to be happy, and if that meant him going to the other end of the earth to be with the man he loved, then so be it.

Chapter 18

Gertrude had managed to find a job as a salesperson in one of the large department stores in Oxford Street. She would meet up with Alice every Friday after work for a night out. They were often chatted up and sometimes went out as a foursome if they happened to meet a couple of congenial men. After George, she could never trust a man again, preferring to remain single, and Alice was enjoying the single life too much to be tied down to one man. She had decided to get rid of George's surname of Bellman and revert to her maiden name of Trent, as then he would never be able to trace her as he had only ever known her by her previous married name of Adams. Gertrude changed her passport back to Trent, and when she bought the flat, she had decided to use that name so that when George was released, he would not be able to find her on the electoral register.

When she had bought her flat after the sale of her house in Kew, she had given half the remainder of the money to Peter, and together with all the money that she had put into a trust fund for him, it was more than enough to set himself up in Perth, Australia. Meanwhile, she and Alice would put money by each week so that they could go on holiday each year to Spain or Greece to get the full benefit of the sun. They thoroughly enjoyed their foreign jaunts together, but after Peter had been living in Australia for a couple of years, he invited Gertrude to come for a visit, and after a little persuasion she agreed to make the long flight to see him.

He had left Wayne's stepmother's hairdressing establishment and found a good position as a stylist in a top salon and Wayne had found a job as a croupier in a casino. It meant working late into the night, but the money was good, and he got plenty of tips. Peter would have preferred him to find a job with more sociable hours, but they were living in a bedsit and saving up for a flat, and for the time being it made sense to put aside as much money as they could.

Eventually, they had saved enough to put a deposit down on a nice little flat overlooking the ocean. When Gertrude arrived, both boys had taken time off to spend with her, showing her the sights and thoroughly spoiling her. They enjoyed barbeques on the beach, spent a day sailing around the harbour, and made several shopping trips with boozy lunches in Perth, but the end of her visit came all too soon. Peter begged her to sell her flat and move to Australia to be near him. "I really, really miss you, Mum," he had told her, "and it would be so great if you lived close by." For a while, she was tempted but then thought about what she would do while the boys were at work. She wouldn't be allowed to take a job, and she didn't know a soul there. She would miss her friends and the good times she shared with Alice. They said a tearful goodbye, promising to Skype each other every week, and she told him that she would save up to visit again after two or three years.

The following year was Peter's thirtieth birthday, and he and Wayne were going out to celebrate at a smart new restaurant overlooking the sea. They had chosen it because it was a place where one could sometimes watch whales swimming out in the bay. The food there was delicious, and the ambience was always warm and welcoming, but disappointingly there were no whales to be seen that day. After they had eaten Wayne gave Peter an elegant gold signet ring for his present and a small box containing an intricately folded piece of paper. "What on earth is this?" asked Peter, amused and intrigued.

"Look, you put your fingers in there and open it this way and then that." Wayne had seen his young sister make one so that she could tell love fortunes at school, and he had asked her to make one for him and that he would write his message inside. When Peter opened the compartments, he read, "Peter will you marry me?" He looked up in amazement as he had not expected that and said delightedly, "Yes, of course, I will!"

The next day, he skyped Gertrude to show off his new ring, and to tell her the good news that he and Wayne were engaged to be married. "We want you and Alice to come over for the wedding, and I'll be sending you the plane tickets next week." Gertrude was thrilled and phoned Alice straight away in excitement. "My goodness, I've never flown further than Spain!" Alice exclaimed. "It's going to be quite an adventure, isn't it?"

"We're going to have to go shopping for our wedding outfits," Gertrude said, and Alice asked, "Are they going to have a formal do or have it on the beach?"

"I haven't the faintest idea," Gertrude said, "but knowing Peter it will probably be on the beach. We'll just have to buy something suitable for either eventuality."

After touring the shops on Oxford Street, they both chose sleeveless dresses that had little matching over jackets. Gertrude had chosen a linen mix in pale green, but Alice had opted for something more colourful and had picked a hot pink dress with a white floral print. Neither of them wanted to wear a hat, but Gertrude had bought a feather fascinator, for as the mother of Peter she felt she should make the effort to look a little more formal.

The flight to Perth seemed endless, and they arrived exhausted. Both Peter and Wayne came to meet them at the airport, and they were all delighted to be reunited once more. The wedding had been arranged for three days after their arrival to give them time to recover from their journey. It was to be held on the beach under a canopy decorated with entwined foliage and exotic flowers.

On their wedding day, both Wayne and Peter were dressed in smart white trousers and shirts that showed off their tans, and Alice murmured to Gertrude, "They look like film stars, don't they?" Wayne's stepmother was dressed in a pretty, flowered silk outfit, and his sister looked beautiful in a fitted blue dress with fresh flowers entwined in her blonde hair. His father did not attend as he just could not come to terms with his son marrying another man. However, he did come to the reception at a smart open-air restaurant because his wife had threatened him and told him that she would not cook for him, nor do his washing, and there would be no sex forthcoming for the foreseeable future. He sat quietly sipping his drink and not joining in the conversation, but Alice made a point of chatting to him, and after a few drinks he opened up and became quite amenable.

Gertrude and Alice had debated what to give the boys for a wedding present. It would have to be something that was not too heavy to carry, and Alice suggested matching cufflinks, but Gertrude said they would probably never wear them. Watches were not right either, as Wayne had received a fine diver's watch from Peter for his thirtieth birthday. Finally, they had decided on matching silver tankards as they both loved their beer, and Gertrude said that even if they didn't use them, they would always look good on the mantlepiece.

There was not enough room in the flat to accommodate both of the women, so Wayne had booked them into a bed and breakfast that was within walking distance from the beach. He had also hired a saloon car for the duration of their stay as his car was a two-seater sports model. They explored the coast road along to Freemantle and enjoyed meals of wonderful, freshly caught seafood. Gertrude and Alice were in their element. "I wish we didn't have to go back" – Alice sighed – "I could happily live out my days here."

"Mum, why don't you make the move here?" Peter asked. "You would be able to stay as my dependant, and Alice could visit every year and stay for a couple of months or so."

"Oh, I don't know if I could bear that journey too often" – Alice laughed – "but it's a nice idea." Wayne thought for a moment or two, and then said, "There is a way you could stay…"

"Really?" Both Alice and Gertrude said in unison.

"Yeah, if you and Gertrude were to get married." Alice burst out laughing and said, "Well, I love Trudy as my dearest friend, but there's no way I'm a lesbian."

"No, I meant just get married for the sake of convenience, and then once you're here you can both go out with blokes to your heart's content."

"It's a good idea," Gertrude said, "and we'll give it some thought." They both discussed it on the journey home, and once they had returned to cold, grey skies, it looked even more tempting, and they began to make serious plans. However, Gertrude was not prepared for what would happen a few weeks later.

Chapter 19

It was after work and Gertrude had just caught the bus in Oxford Street that would take her home to her flat in Chiswick. She was idly looking out of the window when, to her horror, she caught sight of George standing on the pavement. He was waiting to cross the road by Marble Arch tube station, and as she stared in disbelief, he looked up and saw her. She had not been informed by the police that he had been released early, and her blood turned to ice as he glared at her malevolently. To her dismay, she saw that he had managed to hail a cab to follow her.

She did not know what to do, her mind was in turmoil, and when she saw that the bus was about to stop outside Notting Hill tube station, on impulse she leapt off and ran down the steps of the underground. A train had just pulled into the platform, and as the doors opened, she quickened her step and leapt inside. She saw George running after her, but to her relief, the doors closed just a moment before he could get on, and his furious face would haunt her dreams for ages. The train was going in the opposite direction to where she wanted to go, but she got off at Queensway where there were plenty of taxis available. She took a cab to her flat in Chiswick and then locked the door and closed the curtains before collapsing in tears on the bed.

Later, when she had recovered somewhat, she phoned Alice to tell her she had seen George, and what was more to the point, he had seen her and had come after her. Alice reassured her and said that he had no idea where she lived or worked, and to carry on as normal but to keep a wary eye out for him. Gertrude realised the sense of this and was determined to go to work again as usual, and though she kept a constant lookout for George, she didn't see him again and so she began to relax. Then, one day when she was busy re-stocking the shelves with toiletries, a hoarse voice in her ear made her freeze with terror.

"Well, well, so here you are, Gertie," he said smugly. "Did you think I wouldn't find you?"

"What do you want George?" Her throat went dry, and she squeaked, "Leave me alone."

"I think you owe me, don't you Gertie? You owe me big time!"

"I don't owe you anything George. You took all the money I had, and now I've divorced you. I don't want any more to do with you, so please just go and leave me alone."

"Well, that's a shame, I can't do that because I need money, and I know you've got plenty."

"But I haven't got any money," she protested. "Peter had half of everything after I sold my house." He grabbed her arm in a vice-like grip and hissed menacingly, "I lost everything I owned because of you and that bastard son of yours, and if I don't get what I'm owed, then I'll make you sorry you were ever born."

149

Gertrude was shaking with fear, but she had the presence of mind to say, "Alright George, I can give you a bit of cash, but I don't have my card for my savings account with me."

"Then just draw out as much as you can from your current account now," he insisted.

"I can't just leave work," she protested, but he waved aside her objections and said, "Just tell them you'll be taking an early lunch." He stayed with her while she got her bag from her locker, and then took her firmly by the elbow and escorted her to the cashpoint machine. She drew out the maximum daily amount and reluctantly handed it to him and then he told her, "I'll come back tomorrow, so you'd better make sure you have the card for your savings account with you. Otherwise, you're going to be very, very sorry."

Gertrude's legs were shaking as she went back to work, and she told her supervisor that she was feeling ill and needed to go home. She hailed a cab from the rear of the store and went straight home where she locked the door and began to sob hysterically. She would not be able to return to work, that much was clear, because she knew that George would come for her and carry out his threats. Later, she phoned Alice and wailed, "I don't know what to do. He's found me, and I think he means to kill me."

"Well, first things first," Alice said, always practical. "Phone in sick and tell them you've had to quit for personal reasons. Ask them not to give out your address to anyone under any circumstances. Then you need to give your notice formally in writing so that they can give you a reference and send on any wages they owe you."

Gertrude began to write her notice, but she worried that it might be too late, and George would have charmed one of the girls in the office to telling him where she lived. She felt sick, but then suddenly remembered that when she had started working at the store she had still been living with Alice, and it was her address that was on their files. Breathing a sigh of relief, she phoned her friend again and told her that George might turn up on her doorstep. "Destroy any trace of my address," she begged, "and whatever you do, don't tell him where I live," but Alice reassured her and suggested that she lay low for a few days.

When George turned up the following day at Gertrude's place of work, there was no sign of her. He looked around and then asked one of the members of staff where she was, and the woman told him that Gertrude had left. George's brows knitted, and he barked, "What do you mean she's left?"

"She gave in her notice this morning, said something about unforeseen circumstances."

"I'll give her unforeseen circumstances," George muttered under his breath and aloud said, "Where do I go to get her address?"

"I'm afraid we don't give out personal details of members of staff, Sir," the woman said icily.

"But I'm her husband!" George expostulated.

"If she had wanted you to have her address then surely she would have given it to you, Sir," the woman replied before turning on her heel and walking quickly away.

"Bitch!" George muttered. He would have to be a bit more circumspect about tracing Gertrude, and then he remembered that when he'd first seen her she was on a bus heading west, and she had got off at Notting Hill. He took the Central line tube to Notting Hill station and then found a convenient pub, ordered a pint of lager, and asked the landlord if he could borrow his phone directory. "I've lost someone's phone number," he said, "and I know they live somewhere in this area."

There was a public phone by the toilets, so he quickly turned the pages to the B's. There was no one called Bellman, but there were several called Adams. Two of them had the initial G, so he called the first one and a man answered. "Godfrey Adams, how can I help you?"

"Sorry, wrong number," George muttered and then tried his luck with the second one. A quavering female voice answered with, "Hello, who is it?" and George said, "Gertie, is that you?"

"I'm sorry, but I'm a bit deaf," the old woman told him, "can you speak up a bit dear." He slammed the phone down rudely, annoyed that he'd wasted his money on another dead end. He went back to his pint and suddenly he remembered Alice. She was Gertrude's best friend, and she would certainly have her address. "What was her surname?" he wracked his brain and then remembered that it began with a P. Was it Peters? Perry? Petrie? Yes, that was it, Alice Petrie like the Petrie dishes they had used at school.

He turned over the pages of the phone directory until he came to the P's, and there it was! Ms A. Petrie, Flat 17, Parkhurst Mansions, Chiswick, and he punched the air triumphantly. The nearest tube station was Stamford Brook, and George decided he would call on her later that evening. He would not phone her in advance but turn up unannounced about seven o'clock and surprise her. If she worked, she would be home by then, and maybe he would be lucky, and Gertrude would also be there with her. The more he thought about it, the more he was convinced that he would find her at

Alice's place as, after all, women always tended to stick together like glue.

It was just after seven o'clock when George Bellman rang Alice's doorbell. She opened the door, wiping her hands on a tea towel, and looked quite shocked to see him and exclaimed, "George, what on earth are you doing here?"

"Trying to find Gertrude, of course," he said, looking her up and down. "Is she here?"

"No, she isn't," Alice told him, but he barged past her and said, "Well you won't mind if I check for myself then." She thought he had aged a lot and prison had not been kind to him. He had put on quite a bit of weight and looked flabby and out of shape, and had lost that sleek, manicured look that money and power had given him. He now looked jowly with an unhealthy pallor.

"Where is she, Alice?" he demanded. "And don't mess me around. I need to get some money and she owes me big time."

"She hasn't got any money George; she's barely got enough to live on, so there's simply no point in trying to find her."

"That's for me to decide," he snapped and seeing Alice's handbag on the chair he opened it before she could stop him and took out her purse. There were two twenty-pound notes and some loose change, and he took the notes and put them in his pocket. "Put that back!" Alice cried, but he merely said, "Just claim it back from Gertrude."

"I want you to go now," Alice told him firmly, and then he replied, "I will, if you'll just give me her address, and then I'll be out of your hair."

"No!" Alice said forcefully. "She doesn't want you to have it." He came towards her and then she felt a frisson of

153

fear as he grabbed her arm in a vice-like grip and demanded her address book, but she'd had the foresight to rip out the page with Gertrude's address, as she had been warned that George might trace her somehow. She showed him the book and he leafed through it quickly. "What's she listed under?" he demanded, but Alice shrugged and said calmly, "She's not listed."

Suddenly George lost control and slapped Alice hard across the face with enough force to send her reeling across the room so that she hit her face on the corner of the bookcase. His signet ring had caught her when he had hit her, cutting her lip, and she had blood running down her chin. He looked shocked for a moment by what he had done, but only for a moment, and when Alice made a beeline for her mobile phone, he grabbed it before she could pick it up and began to flick through the numbers.

Triumphantly he found Gertrude's numbers listed under the name of Trudy and tapped them into his mobile phone. Seeing that Alice was determined not to give him her address, he decided it would be wise to beat a retreat for the time being, as he could always come back at some later date. "Don't even think of calling the police," he told her, "as I'll be long gone by the time they'd get here."

George had lost control and he hadn't meant to hit Alice, and he'd always thought that men who used violence towards women were despicable, but he had needed to find out where Gertrude lived as he was desperate for money. He had been her husband, and although she had divorced him, he still felt entitled that she owed him his half of the money that she had got for the sale of her house in Kew. If only Alice had been sensible and had handed over the address book then he would never have had to use violence, and he regretted having to hit her as it was Gertrude who was at fault.

He knew that he had been a fool to try and get rid of Peter in the way he did, but if the plan had worked then the drug dealer would have got the blame, and he and Gertrude would still be together. He knew he had been careless, leaving his mobile phone where she could see his messages. If he'd had his time over again, he would have chosen to hold up a post office or two, and then Gertrude would have been none the wiser.

He hoped to God that Alice hadn't called the police as he was only out on license, and any misdemeanour meant that he would have to go back to prison to finish his sentence, and that was not a prospect he relished.

Chapter 20

When George had gone, Alice had to have a stiff drink to calm her nerves and then went to survey the damage in the bathroom mirror. She would be sure to have a lovely black eye in the morning, and her lip was swollen and sore. She phoned Gertrude to say that George had called around demanding to know where she was staying. "I didn't give him your address Trudy, even though he knocked me around a bit," Alice told her, and Gertrude was horrified. "Are you badly hurt?" she asked her friend, but Alice tried to make light of it. "No, just a black eye and a split lip, but I've still got all my teeth. I had to give him your mobile phone number though, and he took my address book, but your home phone is listed under Trent. He doesn't know your maiden name, does he?"

"No, he only knows me as Gertrude Adams."

"Well, if the landline rings in the next couple of days don't answer it. None of my other friends know your address, so you'll be quite safe. Is your mobile registered at your address?"

"No, it's pay as you go," Gertrude told her with relief, "and I don't think that we should meet up for a while just in case he is keeping tabs on you."

"Yes, you could be right," Alice agreed, "he's a nasty piece of work if ever there was one."

"I think you ought to have a chain put on your door, or one of those spy holes so you can see who's calling," Gertrude suggested, as she was worried for her friend in case he should come back. Alice agreed and resolved to call first thing in the morning for a man to come and fit a chain to her door. Later Gertrude's mobile rang, and sure enough, it was George. She told him to get lost in no uncertain terms and cut him off before he could get a word out and then switched off her phone.

Eventually, Gertrude had to go out to stock up on food, and she made sure to buy plenty of non-perishable foodstuffs while keeping a wary eye out for George the whole time. She was overcome with relief to get back home safely, but each time she had to go out she would be convinced that George would find her and do her harm. One day she was certain that she had seen him in the supermarket. She had her first panic attack, and then one of the members of staff had taken her into the back room and calmed her down before calling a taxi to take her home. It was not George she had seen, just someone who resembled him, but it was the start of her fear of going out.

George had followed Alice on several occasions, sure that she would eventually lead him to Gertrude. She had suspected that he would do that and had kept well away, only communicating with her friend on the phone. He had been desperate for money, and so with the couple of hundred pounds that he had taken from Gertrude's cash point, he had gone straight to the casino. There he found that a new manager was now in charge who didn't know him, and who had not wanted to admit him as he looked rather shabby, but George had a life membership and insisted on going in, and so the manager could not refuse him entry.

He had headed straight for the Black-Jack table, as he had always thought that playing Roulette was for fools who didn't care if they lost their money. His luck had been in, and he had won that evening, doubling his money, and so he decided to look up a few of his old pals. First on his list was Lenny, but his old friend was not too pleased to see him. He had retired from all the crooked deals and just wanted to live a quiet life. To get rid of him, he gave him a couple of hundred, and then George set off for Soho to some of his old haunts in the hope of reconnecting with some of his old dealers.

The next time that Gertrude set out to buy her food, she got as far as the end of her street, and then her heart began to pound, and she struggled to breathe, and she thought she was having a heart attack. Eventually, she calmed down, but she headed back home and did not feel better until she had closed the front door behind her. It happened again the following time she tried to go to the shops, and in despair, she phoned Alice and begged her to get some food shopping. Her friend brought enough to keep her stocked up for quite a few days and delivered it to her in a taxi. This now would follow a pattern, as each time that Gertrude attempted to go anywhere it would bring on another panic attack, and even thinking about going out brought on a feeling of stress.

Alice tried several times to make her friend go out, but it was no good. Gertrude just could not bear to be away from the safety of her flat. Her only pleasure and link with the outside world was her weekly Skype to Peter in Australia, and she wished heartily that she had taken up his offer to move there with him. He was very happy, and both he and Wayne were doing well, so in order not to worry him, she did not tell him that she had seen George or that she was now too terrified to leave the house.

Every Friday, Alice would bring over her shopping and they would share a bottle of wine and a takeaway, but it could never again be like the old days when they went dancing or to the cinema. Gertrude's days now revolved around the television, and so she was delighted when Sam and Jessica moved into the vacant flat upstairs. Jess often popped in for a cup of tea and a chat, and when Josh was born Gertrude would babysit for them with pleasure.

One day, Alice arrived midweek in a state of excitement and asked if she had seen the papers. "No, why?" Gertrude asked, curious to know why her friend was being so mysterious. Alice showed her the article, and Gertrude read that the police had found the body of a man in an alleyway in Soho. He had been stabbed and had later been identified as a petty criminal, George Bellman. "You're free now Trudy!" Alice cried. "He is gone forever, and he can't hurt you anymore."

That evening George had headed to a drinking club that he'd used to frequent before his spell in jail, and there he had met up with a couple of his old acquaintances. He'd not noticed the man who was watching him and who was a pal of the drug dealer that he owed money to. He had followed George, who had then gone to visit a prostitute, and when he came out the dealer was waiting for him in a dark alley. "Got a light mate?" he'd asked, and as George had got out his lighter, he'd thrust a knife between his ribs, and George fell dying in a filthy Soho gutter.

Gertrude was stunned. She read the article again, just to make sure it was him, and when it finally sunk in that George was dead and she was free of him at last. "Come on Trudy, get your glad-rags on," Alice urged. "We're going out to celebrate!" Gertrude walked to her dressing table in a kind of dream and began to put on some make-up and do her hair, and it felt so strange to be getting ready to go out again. Alice poured them both a glass of wine and then helped her choose an outfit. They decided they would go to their local Italian restaurant to celebrate her freedom, but she had only taken a few steps along the road when all the old panic-stricken feelings came back, and she had to run back to the house.

"I don't understand it, Trudy," Alice said in despair, "because you're not in danger anymore so why can't you leave the house?"

"I don't know," Gertrude wept, "I really want to go out, but somehow I just can't do it."

She was never able to leave the house again, and her life became more and more restricted once the power cuts began.

Chapter 21

It was soon to be the day of Wayne's fortieth birthday, and Peter had wracked his brains as to what to get him. It was after all a milestone birthday, and he would have to find something suitable to mark the occasion. Wayne already had a nice watch, so that was not an option, and there was nothing that he liked to collect. Then, on one of their days out to the beach, Wayne had mentioned that he would love to learn how to scuba dive, and now Peter had the perfect present. A wet suit and a course of lessons would delight him, and maybe next holiday they could fly up to the Great Barrier Reef.

After breakfast on Wayne's birthday, Peter presented him with a huge box carefully wrapped in striped paper, and he looked rather surprised and asked, "What's this?"

"Open it and see," Peter laughed, and he managed to capture on camera the look of delight on Wayne's face when he saw what was inside. They had booked the same restaurant that evening overlooking the sea where they had spent Peter's thirtieth birthday, and this time they were lucky enough to spot some whales out in the bay. Then, full of wine and lobster and feeling amorous, they headed home to their flat, but as they opened the door, the phone rang. It was the housekeeper from Wayne's uncle's hotel, and she said, "Wayne, I'm so sorry to have to be the one to tell you bad news, but I'm afraid your uncle has passed away."

"Oh no! Poor Uncle Tim, what happened?"

"It was a heart attack. He'd not been feeling too well for a couple of weeks, but he wouldn't go to the doctor, you know what he thought of them. I've arranged the funeral for next Friday if that's okay with you, and I need to know if you're able to come."

"Yes, of course, I'll book a flight tomorrow and I'll let you know when I'm arriving, so please keep a room free for me."

Peter asked him what had happened, and Wayne replied, "My uncle Tim, Mum's brother, has died. He lived up in Cairns where he owned a small hotel."

"I'm so sorry, I hope it hasn't ruined your night?"

"No, don't be silly. I haven't seen Uncle Tim for ten years. He was always so busy, but we spoke on the phone from time to time. I don't know what's going to happen about the hotel."

The next morning, Wayne booked his flight and took a week off work, and Peter had asked if he wanted him to go with him, but he had said no. The airfare was expensive and there would most likely be a lot of boring stuff to sort out once he arrived.

Peter phoned Gertrude to tell her that Wayne's uncle had died, and he would be flying up to Cairns for the funeral. "What did you get him for his birthday?" Gertrude asked, "and did he get my card in time?"

"Yes, he got the card, Mum, and he thanks you for remembering. I got him some scuba diving lessons and a wet suit, and he was thrilled, and I'll send you a photo of him wearing it."

He told her they had spent Wayne's birthday at the same restaurant where they had celebrated his thirtieth birthday, and this time they had seen the whales. He was a little worried about his mother, as she had not seemed too well the last time that he had been able to Skype her, and her face had looked very pale despite the make-up she wore. He had been touched to see that she'd had her hair done in a new style, courtesy of one of Alice's friends. He asked if she was feeling quite well, but she had assured him that she was fine. "You'll have to go out in the sun a bit more," he had said, but she had laughed and said, "Yeah once it stops raining." She had never told him what had happened to her with George, and he had no idea that she was now unable to leave the house.

When Wayne returned from Cairns, he could barely contain his excitement. Peter met him at the airport and asked how the funeral had gone. "It was lovely," Wayne told him, "and very moving, and he had a lot of his old friends there who told me stories about him, he was quite a character, and then we laid him to rest in the churchyard next to my Aunt Gwen. Anyway, I have something amazing to tell you. You are now looking at a new hotel owner!"

"Really?" Peter looked at him in surprise. "Yeah," Wayne grinned, "Uncle Tim left me the whole works. The hotel isn't that big, but it's in a beautiful place, surrounded by palm trees and with views of the sea on two sides. Here, I'll show you." He showed Peter the pictures on his mobile phone, and he had to agree that it looked just like paradise.

"What have you decided to do? Are you going to take it on, or will you sell it?" Peter asked, and Wayne said, "It all depends on what you think. I would love to give it a go, but if you'd rather not make the move, I'd understand."

"Wayne, it's a no-brainer!" Peter told him, "I'd love to move to Cairns with you. It'll be such an adventure!"

"That's great, and you could even have your salon on the premises if you like. We'd have our very own luxury villa on the grounds."

"I can't wait!" Peter responded enthusiastically and asked Wayne when he planned to go.

"As soon as possible. I thought maybe we could buy a camper van, pack up all our stuff and drive across the country. Let's make a sort of holiday of it, how does that grab you?"

"That would be great. I've always wanted to see more of Australia."

The day soon dawned when they were to set off on their drive across the outback to Cairns, and Peter had written a long letter to Gertrude to let her know what they had planned, and Wayne had printed off a couple of photos of the hotel and views to show her. "I'll let you know my new address when we get there," Peter had written, "and I'm going to have my own salon. I thought of calling it 'To Dye For'. What do you think? Not too cheesy, is it?"

Gertrude had laughed when she read that, and she had a warm glow of pride to think that her boy would now have his own business and be master of his destiny. The hotel grounds had looked so beautiful, and she mentally cursed herself for not emigrating to Australia when she had the chance, but it was just the thought of leaving her best friend Alice behind that had coloured her decision to stay in London.

Wayne suggested that they should sell all their furniture as there would be no need for it once they reached the hotel, so they only packed their clothes and a few favourite prints and books, and only one or two ornaments that they didn't want to part with. They then advertised the contents of their flat for sale on the internet and soon almost everything had gone, and the few things that were behind left they gave to a charity shop.

They said goodbye to Wayne's father, stepmother, and not-so-little sister, who was now in her twenties and attending teacher's training college. "Can I come up and visit you in the holidays?" she asked, and Wayne said, "Sure, as long as you help out a bit. Once I'm flush, I'll send you the airfare." His father formally shook hands with him and rather grudgingly wished him luck, and ignored Peter, but his stepmother and sister Lily gave them both a hug and wished them God speed. Peter could not understand how a father could not embrace his son. Did he think being gay was catching? He wondered how his father would have reacted to the knowledge that his only son was gay. From what he remembered of Roy, he would most likely have been fine about it. Wayne didn't seem bothered, he'd not expected a last-minute change of heart, and, in his eyes, he saw it as his father's loss.

Wayne and Peter set off on their epic journey full of hope and high spirits. Peter had never learnt to drive, as his place of work had been a short bus ride from their flat, so the driving fell to Wayne, and it meant that they had to make quite a several stops so that he could take a rest. From Perth they headed for Kalgoorlie where they stocked up with more supplies, making sure to pack plenty of bottles of water, as they would be crossing a vast expanse of desert before they reached Alice Springs. Once there, they had planned to take a few days break to rest and relax, before continuing on their long journey to Cairns.

A couple of days out of Kalgoorlie Peter moaned, "I think we should have taken the coast road, don't you? There's nothing much in the way of scenery, is there?"

"You were the one who wanted to see Australia" – Wayne shrugged – "and I think we were probably crazy to decide to drive all that way, especially as I'm the one doing all the work."

They were tetchy with each other for the rest of the day, but that night they slept under the stars and made up their spat. "I've never seen so many stars," Peter said, gazing up in wonder at the night sky, "and it's so quiet here, you can almost hear the earth moving." Wayne grinned and said, "I'm glad I can still do it for you mate!"

They set off early the next day so that they could escape the worst of the heat, and at lunchtime, they rested in the shade of the van and drank a couple of beers. After a short nap, they set off again, but Wayne felt very weary, and his shoulders were stiff and aching from all that driving. The road ahead was quite straight and there had been no traffic apart from one lorry that had passed them ages ago, so he decided that they had to share the driving.

"Peter, I think it's time you took over the wheel," Wayne said firmly, but Peter protested, "But I can't, you know I don't know how to drive."

"It's easy, just keep your foot on the accelerator and keep her straight." He showed him the brake and the clutch and said, "I'll change gear for you, just do as I say, and you'll be fine."

They changed places and Peter nervously took the wheel. "Now put your right foot on the accelerator and your left foot on the clutch and gently press down and I'll change gears."

After a couple of false starts, Peter managed to get the hang of it, and then began to enjoy the experience. He began to increase his speed, but Wayne said, "Don't go too fast, as this old girl isn't built for speed." Suddenly one of the front tyres blew out, and the van slewed all over the road. Peter had no idea what to do, but Wayne grabbed the wheel and yelled for him to brake. He braked, but too hard, and the van skidded out of control, hit a rock, and overturned, tumbling down over and over into a steep ravine.

When Peter regained consciousness, he could not move. He was thoroughly wedged behind the wheel, and every time he tried to lift himself out, he was hit by a wave of such excruciating pain that he screamed in agony. He called out for Wayne, but his partner had been thrown through the windscreen and was dead. "Someone will find us," he thought, but the hours passed, and nobody came. He had a terrible thirst, and he could see the water bottle lying on the floor, just out of his reach. Peter was in despair and tried desperately to call someone on his mobile phone, but here, in the outback, there was no signal. He began to realise that Wayne was dead, as there had been no sound or movement from him whatsoever, and he prayed that his end would come soon.

After a while, he began to hallucinate and to think that Wayne was looking at him through the broken windscreen of the van. Then he thought he could see his mother looking at him and called out, but it was just his reflection in the wing mirror. After another couple of hours had passed it was starting to grow dark, and then he saw Wayne again, he was holding out his hand to him and saying, "Come on Peter, I'm waiting for you," and so he reached out and took Wayne's hand, and then his soul left his body, and he was free. Soon vultures had begun to circle over the ravine, but no one thought anything of them, because no one had yet realised that the two young men were missing.

A few weeks later, Wayne's stepmother received a call from the manageress of the hotel in Cairns asking if she had heard anything from the two men. "No, not a word, but I expect they've stopped off somewhere for a bit of a break." She asked, "There's no hurry, is there?"

"Not really, only I had expected them to arrive two weeks ago, and Wayne hasn't been in contact at all. What do you think I should do, just carry on as before?"

"Yes, I think that's probably best, and I shouldn't worry too much. I'm guessing that he can't get a signal on his mobile phone, and he'll show up in his own good time."

Eight months later, a lorry driver on his way to Alice Springs stopped at the roadside to relieve himself and saw the van lying at the bottom of the ravine. Overcome with curiosity, he clambered down to investigate, and to his horror found the remains of the two young men. As soon as he was able to get a signal on his phone, he called the police, who then sent a helicopter to search for the site. They had been looking for them, as Wayne's stepmother had finally reported them missing several weeks after they had disappeared, but without success. Now they were able to recover what was left of the bodies and ascertain their identities. Wayne's family was informed that he had been found after what seemed to be a tragic accident. They had contacted the British police with the details for Peter's next of kin, but Gertrude was never to know what had happened to him.

Chapter 22

Alice's death had shocked Gertrude deeply, and now she realised that there was no one left to care about her. She wondered what her son Peter and his partner were doing. Perhaps they were spending the holidays on the beach, but she had not heard from him for almost a year. She used to be able to Skype him, and he had kept in touch regularly, but that system had come to an end for the time being, and for the last couple of years, she'd only received about half a dozen letters from him.

The last time she had heard from him he had been so excited, telling her that Wayne had received a legacy. His uncle, who lived up in Cairns, had died and left him a small hotel in his will. They were going to pack up all their belongings, buy a camper van and drive up there, planning their route across the country. They were both looking forward to the adventure, and both Peter and Wayne were sad that Gertrude and Alice could not fly out to join them for the grand re-opening. "I wish you could both be with us, Mum, but I know it's just not possible," he had written. "I'll send our new address as soon as we get there, and I'll send you lots of photos of our new home."

She had written several times since his last letter but had received no reply, not even a card, and he was impossible to contact. She had tried everything, even writing to the Australian embassy, but to no avail, and on New Year's Eve, she came to a decision.

She had spent that Christmas Day alone, but thankfully the electricity had been on. She'd been able to microwave a turkey meal for one and then watch a film on television, but now it was dark most of the time and she'd simply had enough. That afternoon she prepared her will and wrote two letters. One was to her son, Peter, and the other was to Jess. She suddenly realised that she would have to get the will witnessed, but it meant having to go outside to the basement flat where the Romanian couple lived. They were not very friendly, never mixing with anyone, but she knew that they could speak English because she had heard the woman shouting at the dustmen when they had made a mess.

Gathering all her courage, she opened the front door and stood on the threshold hesitating for a moment or two. Then, holding on to the wall for dear life, she limped as fast as she could and went down the steps to the basement and rang the doorbell. After a few moments, the door opened a crack and the women said curtly, "Yes, what do you want?"

"Please," Gertrude said, "I'm so sorry to bother you on New Year's Eve, but I need your help with something very important."

"Okay, you better come in," The Romanian woman motioned her in impatiently and then closed the door behind her. "I've written out my will," Gertrude said, "and I need both you and your husband to witness my signature."

"What is will? I not understand." The woman frowned, and Gertrude explained, "It's for when I'm dead, who I want to have my things."

"Ah okay." The woman comprehended and said, "I will get my husband." She left Gertrude standing in the hallway. There was no offer of a glass of sherry or even a cup of tea, but then she had not expected anything, just maybe hoped for a little congenial company on this the last day of the year. The woman returned after a couple of minutes with her husband, and then they both stood over her watching as she wrote her signature, and then they both signed and dated it below. "Thank you so much," Gertrude said with relief, "and I'm sorry to have bothered you today. Happy New Year!" The woman had the grace to look a little abashed, and she watched as Gertrude climbed painfully up the steps, and then called out, "Happy New Year," before closing the door firmly behind her.

Gertrude hurried back inside and, once she had closed her front door, she breathed a sigh of relief. What she was about to do, she had been taught was a great sin and she would end in purgatory, but she thought, "Well, I'm in purgatory now, and it can't be any worse than this." She had been in constant pain for months and urgently needed a hip replacement, and her eyesight had now deteriorated so that she could not read for long without getting a headache. However, it was the loneliness and the long hours of darkness that she could no longer bear.

Because it was New Year's Eve, the power stayed on until half-past twelve, and Gertrude decided to turn on the TV. She made a pot of tea then and finished off the box of chocolates that Maria, her home help, had given her for Christmas. Then, bored with the programmes, she got up and looked again at the three cards she had received and that stood on her mantelpiece. The one that Jess had given her showed a beautiful winter landscape, and there was a nativity scene from Maria and then a funny one from Alice, and as she read her friend's good wishes she began to weep. It was beginning to get colder now, and as Gertrude went to close the curtains she saw with amazement that it had begun to snow.

Suddenly she felt elated. It was the perfect ending. She had always loved the snow as a young girl, but it had been years since it had fallen in the city. She filled a hot water bottle and put it in her bed and then fetched the half bottle of brandy that she had left over from the previous Christmas. She had kept it for medicinal reasons, not liking the taste, but it would do to serve her purpose. On her bedside table was a bottle containing five sleeping tablets that she had been saving, and then she turned her radio on to the classical music station and got into bed.

To the strains of Elgar's Enigma Variations, she took the tablets one by one and washed them down with a mouthful of the brandy. After she had swallowed the final tablet, she lay back and watched the snowflakes swirling down, and then after a while, it seemed as if she was flying up to the sky. *"How strange,"* she thought, and then her eyes closed for the last time and her soul left her body and floated upwards towards the heavens.

Chapter 23

Jess had been devastated at the way the manager had treated her. She felt strongly that she did not deserve to be fired for something that wasn't her fault. He didn't even have the courtesy to hear her out. She had always been a diligent worker and so she would make sure to contact the union to see if she had a reasonable case to fight against her dismissal.

She stopped at the corner shop to buy some bread, milk, and some pasta for her supper, and then wearily made her way home. As she passed the deserted factory where the feral cats lived, she was concerned to see that some demolition equipment had been moved in and workmen were starting to clear the site. She could see no sign of the cats, and she hoped that they had been rescued by the RSPCA, or maybe they had just moved on to pastures new.

She felt bone-weary and her back ached, and she longed for her bed, but as she approached the flat she saw an undertaker's van parked outside. Quickening her steps, she was in time to see them bring out a body on a covered trolley and she called out, "Who's died?"

"It's the old lady from the ground floor flat," the man told her.

"Oh no, not Mrs Trent. What happened?"

"I don't know Miss," the undertaker said, and then added, "The police are inside." Jess went in and finding Gertrude's door ajar, knocked and entered nervously. A police constable was there along with Gertrude's social worker and Maria, who looked white and shaken.

"Who are you?" The police constable demanded, and Jess replied, "I live on the first floor flat; my name is Jessica Jones. What's happened to Mrs Trent?"

"It looks as if she took her own life," the home-help, Maria told Jess. "She was so lonely, especially after her friend Alice died."

"Oh no, poor soul." Jess brushed a tear from her eye and said, "I did ask her to come and stay with us for Christmas, but she was too afraid to leave the house."

"Yes, I know, she hasn't been outside for years. I used to get all her shopping for her, and I reckon that she must have been in so much pain from her hip," Maria confided, "but she wouldn't even think of letting me take her to the doctor's surgery."

Maria had been a little late arriving at Gertrude's flat on the second of January. It was almost ten-thirty as she unlocked the door, and she thought that the flat was too quiet. She wondered if the old lady was still asleep, and so she began by tidying the living room, not that it needed much tidying, just running a duster around and plumping up the cushions. Then, as the electricity was working, she put the kettle on to make Gertrude a cup of tea.

She tapped on her bedroom door, and getting no reply went in, calling, "Morning Gertrude, I've brought you a cuppa." There was no response, so with a sudden sinking feeling in the pit of her stomach, she approached the figure lying in the bed. Gertrude's eyes were open and angled towards the window, where the curtains had been pulled back, and when Maria touched her face, her skin felt stone cold.

The cup of tea slipped from her grasp, and her hand flew to her mouth. It was then that she saw the empty bottle of sleeping pills on the bedside table, and the empty bottle of brandy that had partly rolled under the bed. "Holy Mother, no!" she cried and crossed herself as she realised that Gertrude's death had not been natural but suicide. Maria was a devout Catholic, and she had been brought up to believe that to commit suicide was a mortal sin, and those souls would spend eternity in purgatory, and so she said a heartfelt prayer for Gertrude's soul, and then she called the police.

"Do you know if she had any relatives?" The constable asked Jess, who nodded and said, "Yes, she had a son in Australia, but I don't think that she'd heard from him for quite a long time, and I don't believe she had his new address."

She took her leave and struggled upstairs to her flat with the heavy trolley. She had brought Gertrude back some honey and eggs from home and she felt sad that her friend would not get to enjoy them. She shed a few tears thinking about poor Gertrude being all on her own over the holidays and then ultimately deciding to put an end to her lonely life, but she didn't blame her.

It was a couple of months later that Jess received a call from Gertrude's solicitor, asking her to come to his office at eleven o'clock the following morning as he had some information that would be of interest to her. She was intrigued and thought perhaps that she had been left a little money by her friend. It would certainly come in very useful, as she had been desperately looking for another job, but so far, she had not even been asked for an interview.

She arrived promptly at eleven the following morning to find that Maria, the home help, was already waiting in reception. "Hello, have you come to hear Mrs Trent's will?" she asked Jess, who nodded and took the seat next to her. After a couple of minutes, the solicitor came out and asked them to step into his office. "I have here Mrs Gertrude Trent's last will, and she has left you both a legacy. To Maria Jenner, I leave the sum of £2000 with my thanks for all her care, and I also leave her the blue glass vase that she had always admired. To my dear friend Jessica Jones, I leave my flat and all the contents, and the sum of £1000. To my beloved son, Peter, I leave the rest of my money to be held in a savings account, but if he doesn't claim it within five years then the money is to go to Jessica Jones."

Jess gasped and then burst into tears. The solicitor looked up in surprise over his glasses and asked, "Are you alright Mrs Jones? Would you like a glass of water?" Jess nodded and after a moment or two, she became calm once more. "I'm so sorry," she said, feeling rather embarrassed by her outburst, "but it was the shock. I never expected anything like that, and it couldn't have come at a better time, because I lost my job recently and I haven't been able to find another one."

"Well, you won't have to worry now, will you?" Maria said, feeling more than a little envious. "Come on, let's go to the pub and you can buy me a drink to celebrate."

Later, as soon as she had returned home, Jessica phoned Sam. He had been very upset that she had lost her job as they had relied on her salary. He also felt that she had been wrongly dismissed as no one could have predicted the severity of the snowstorm that night.

"Sam, you'll never guess what's happened," she began. But he interrupted her, "Don't tell me, you've found a job already?"

"No, it's much better than that," Jess said excitedly. "You won't believe this, Sam, but I've become an heiress!"

"What on earth are you on about?" Sam laughed.

"Gertrude had made a will and she left me her flat and all the contents!"

"But that means…"

"…I can come home for good! I've already decided that I'm going to move into her flat while I redecorate our place, and then I'll put it on the market. It doesn't need anything much doing to it, and I'm pretty sure it will sell very quickly. What do you think?"

"I think that's perfect," Sam agreed, "and once you've done up her flat, we could rent it out to bring in some income."

"You don't want me to sell it then?"

"No, as we'll have more than enough to live on," he assured her, "and it will be there for Josh when he's older if ever he wants to move to London." Josh had been very upset to learn of Gertrude's death as she had been like a grandmother to him, more so than Sam's mother, as he had spent so much of his formative years in her company. He had missed her when they had moved away. Now Jess could imagine the look of sheer delight on his face when Sam got to tell him that Gertrude had left his mum enough money so that she could come home and never have to go back to the city.

The solicitor had given Jess the keys to Gertrude's flat and now she went downstairs and opened the door. It smelt a bit musty and as she looked around, she realised that it would take her at least a couple of weeks to get it into a fit state to be rented out. On the bedside table was an envelope and she saw that it was addressed to her. She picked it up and took it back upstairs and while the electricity was still on, made herself a cup of tea and put a pasta bake in the oven, and then she sat down at the table and opened the letter and read;

My Dear Jess,

I hope you forgive me for taking the easy way out, but I'd had enough. After Alice died, I had no one left who knew me from my youth and who knew what I'd been through. You have been very kind to me, and when you and Sam moved in I was so pleased, especially as you always had time for a cup of tea and a chat. It meant a lot. When Josh was born, it was lovely to have a young child around the house again, and I did love babysitting for you. I missed him so much when he moved to the countryside with Sam, but I know what a terrible wrench it was for you and now you can all be together once more.

Your friend, Gertrude.

Jess was moved to tears by Gertrude's letter. She had not had any conception of just how lonely and empty her life had been, and that she had clung to Jess's friendship as a small beacon of light in her otherwise grey and drab existence.

After she had spoken to Sam, she went to bed to mull over what she would do next. She was too excited to sleep and tried to imagine how her life would be once the money came through. Sam would have told Josh the good news by now, and she tried to visualise his look of delight as he realised that he would soon have his mum home for good. She had an overwhelming desire to hold him close, but she would have to be patient for just a little while longer.

The next morning, there was no need to get up early for work, so Jess lay in bed and waited for the electricity to come on, and then she switched on the immersion heater so that she could have a hot, leisurely bath. While she waited for the water to heat up she made tea and toast which she spread generously with the honey that she'd brought from home. Once she had bathed and dressed, she went downstairs and began to clear out Gertrude's flat.

There were an awful lot of books, and she started with these and began sorting them into two piles, the ones she wanted to keep, and the majority that was destined to go to the charity shop. She had soon filled her trolley and realised that it would take her several trips to get everything cleared. There were also a lot of knick-knacks and ornaments, mainly figurines of crinoline ladies and china dogs, and these she would wrap carefully in newspaper ready to take down to the charity shop. There were, however, a couple of attractive vases that she would hang on to, and a very pretty Tiffany-style lamp which she would take home to the cottage. It would look perfect there, and she had just the place in mind for it to light up a dark corner.

After three trips to the charity shop, Jess treated herself to lunch and half a bottle of wine at a local Italian bistro and then went to buy some paint and brushes, so that she could make a start on the decorating. She decided to begin in the spare bedroom, as she didn't fancy the idea of sleeping in the bed where Gertrude had died, and once that was completed she could move downstairs and put her flat upstairs on the market.

The small wardrobe and chest of drawers in the spare room had quite enough space to house her meagre collection of clothes. They were empty apart from a few of Peter's old, discarded things that were too shabby to donate anywhere but the dustbin. Then she swept and dusted the room, thoroughly scrubbed and disinfected the bathroom. Utterly exhausted, Jess went back to her bed and immediately fell into a deep, dreamless sleep.

The next morning, feeling refreshed and raring to go, she painted the spare room and the bathroom and then turned out all the cupboards in the kitchen. She had half expected to find mice but was relieved that there seemed to be no sign of any rodent droppings anywhere. Everything was scrubbed until it gleamed, and then she began to move her clothes down to the wardrobe and chest of drawers in the spare room. She then spent her last night in her old flat and could not help feeling a little nostalgic for the good times she'd had there with Sam and little Josh. She told herself not to be silly, and that the best times were yet to come.

The following morning Jess moved the last few of her items into the downstairs flat and then, checking that her old place was clean and looking as inviting as it possibly could, she made a trip to the estate agents to tell them that she had a flat to sell. On her return, she saw that the postman had called and there were a couple of bills on the mat for Gertrude. She would have to remember to write to them as soon as possible and inform them that she was now the new owner of the flat and get them to change everything into her name. As she sorted through the post, she found a letter addressed to Mrs Adams and it had an Australian stamp. She was just about to put 'not known at this address' when she suddenly remembered that Gertrude's first husband had been Adams and that it was also Peter's surname. Gertrude had changed her name back to her maiden name of Trent so that she could escape George's clutches.

Jess turned the envelope over in her hands and wondered if she should open it. She went inside and sat on the bed and then thought maybe it was from Peter and that she would now have to inform him that his mother had died, so she tore it open and took out the letter.

It was not from Gertrude's son but had an official logo, and she saw that it was from the Queensland Police asking Gertrude to contact her local police station and to show them this letter. Jess went to the police station first thing the following morning, and after a while, a woman detective took her into a side room and asked her to sit down.

"Are you Mrs Adams?"

"No, my name is Jessica Jones, and Mrs Adams, or Trent as she was known by, has died recently and left all her property to me. I know she has a son in Australia, Peter Adams, but she hadn't heard from him in quite a while." The policewoman then told her that they had found the body of her son and another young man in the wreck of a vehicle in a remote quarry. The van must have been there for some months, and the only clue as to how the accident had happened was a burst tyre, but the documents found in one of the cases were those of Peter Adams. Jess let out a long breath as she realised that she would now come into even more money and that she would have to inform the solicitor as soon as possible.

The following week Jess was busy showing prospective buyers around her upstairs flat and one couple had asked to see the place again. They were in their thirties with a small toddler, and Jess was reminded of her and Sam when they had first moved into the flat, in what seemed like a lifetime ago. They had liked the flat, but they didn't have much money and wanted to try and reduce the price, and because she liked them and felt they would be good neighbours, Jess agreed. She also paid a visit to the solicitor to show him the letter she had received from the Australian Police. He said he would have to confirm it, but it looked very likely that she would soon get the remainder of Gertrude's money, and it was quite a considerable sum.

A month later, Jess heard from the solicitor, and she was delighted to find that Gertrude's legacy had been worth £45,000. The sale of the flat also went through smoothly, the deposit having been paid, and the rest would be due in six weeks when the young couple was due to move in. Jess could then move back to the countryside to be with Sam and Josh, just as soon as she had managed to let the downstairs flat. She then remembered that a couple of her old workmates had been looking for accommodation nearer to their work, and she decided to visit them. She waited until lunchtime, and then made her way up to her old office and they were delighted to see her again and told her that they had not been able to find anywhere suitable in the area. Just then the manager walked in, looked Jess up and down, and sneered, "Well, well, well, if it isn't Mrs Jones. If you've come begging for your old job back, I'm afraid you're going to be disappointed, as we've already found a replacement for you."

"I wouldn't want your lousy job for all the tea in China," Jess said tartly, giving him a hard look, and was gratified to see him go red and turn sharply on his heel. "Come on girls," she said cheerfully, "I'll treat you to lunch in the pub and you can come and see the flat after work."

Jess had now finished all the decorating, having left Gertrude's bedroom until last. The room still retained her presence, and she felt as if she had no right to be going through her personal things. Telling herself that she was being silly she made a start by emptying the chest of drawers, but most of the clothing there was too worn out and had to be thrown away.

In a leather box, on top of the chest, were a few items of jewellery, and among them was an expensive-looking pair of diamond earrings that had been designed to look like dollar signs. They didn't look as if they belonged to Gertrude, not being her style at all. They had been left behind at Alice's flat after George had pawned all her jewellery. Alice had borrowed them for a special date, but Gertrude had never really liked them and had never worn them again. The rest of the other jewellery was quite understated, but she knew that she would get a good amount of money for the diamond earrings at the jewellers in the high street.

Jess then found Gertrude's marriage certificates and her birth certificate. She was quite shocked to see that she had only been in her early seventies because she had looked well into her eighties.

The wardrobe was stuffed full of dresses but hidden at the bottom was a photo album. Jess opened it, and as she leafed through it she could see that Gertrude had been very beautiful in her youth and she had made such a lovely bride. Her first husband had looked kind, and she could see the resemblance to Peter. There had been countless photos of the young lad growing up. There was only one photo of George, however, and it had been scribbled over, and Jess thought that he'd been quite a handsome man in a rough and ready kind of way, but she didn't much like his cold eyes. They made her shiver, and she could see why Gertrude had later become so afraid of him.

As she began to take out and pack away the clothes, Jess noticed a bright red silk evening dress hanging at the back of the wardrobe. She pulled it out and held it up to herself in the full-length mirror, and the colour suited her. It was very tempting, and she simply could not resist trying it on. She found that it fitted her slim figure perfectly. Wearing the dress, she looked and felt amazing, just like one of those film stars in the old movies that Gertrude had always loved to watch.

Jess turned in front of the mirror, admiring herself from every angle, and tried to imagine what Gertrude would have looked like in the dress. She was blonde in those days, of course, but red would have suited her just as well, and she would most likely have received no end of compliments. She walked over to the bed and picked up the photo album and there, tucked in at the back, were two snapshots of her wearing it. One of them showed her on her own, and she was laughing and posing in the manner of a film star, and the other was of her together with her friend Alice, which they must have asked the salesgirl to take for them. They both looked so young and pretty, and she felt such sadness for the little grey-haired, bent old lady that she had become, and for her lonely and isolated existence.

Jess went back to the mirror to have a last look at her reflection, and she knew that she would probably never go anywhere smart enough to wear it, but she could not bear to take the dress to the charity shop. Folding it carefully, she packed it away in her case and wondered what Sam would say when he saw it. He would most probably think she was mad, but it was a beacon of hope to her, a hope that someday things would get better, and that they would be able to come out of the dark into a brighter future.